DEAD ORPHANS

DEAD ORPHANS

Dead Orphans:

A Collection of Dark Short Fiction

Book Cover by Bert Edens

First Printing, 2024

ISBN-13: 979-8-8690-9359-2

Dedication

I could not have done this without Carrie, My Gorgeous Bride. Not only is she my alpha reader and gets to be the first to see the warped ideas spawned by my weird brain, she is also the one who continues to encourage and push me. When she asks me what's wrong with me, I both worry and know my stories are on the right track. Thank you for always supporting and being there for me, Darlin'. I love you.

Table of Contents

Preface

I hate coming up with titles. I love writing. I tolerate editing. But I hate the process of figuring out the title for a piece. I'll write and edit and perfect and send to beta readers and finish my final edits. Then I'll come up with a title, if only because I have to.

For whatever reason, the title of this collection, *Dead Orphans*, long predated the compilation of the stories. I knew I wanted to gather stories I'd written that had never found a home, whether I had tried or not. They were literary orphans, and saying they were dead, well, that just fit the theme of the collection.

There are a variety of stories in this collection, ranging in length from a tweet to a lengthy short story. Not all are horror, but all are dark, and many are disturbing, depressing, or even shocking.

The majority of my writing, in terms of sheer numbers, has been on Twitter/X. There are many daily prompts of a single word, and the goal is to write a tweet-length story using that word as the inspiration. So in those tweets, you'll see "#vss365", which stands for Very Short Story, and the prompts are 365 days a year. The word for the day will also be prefixed with an octothorpe. Didn't know that had a name, did you?

While I haven't done many of them, I did include a couple drabbles, which are stories that are exactly 100 words in length. It's something I want to play with more.

Something I love about tweets, and by extension drabbles or other micro-fiction with extreme word limits, is you have to practice word economy. It helps you look at a sentence and decide, how could it be reworded so it's not as lengthy? Are there any unnecessary or repetitive words? Can I find a more powerful word that also happens to be shorter? All of this is a great exercise to tighten up your writing.

I hope you enjoy this collection of literary babies, offspring who until now were homeless. Maybe you'll want to adopt one and make it your favorite.

Bert Edens
bert@bert-edens.com

Dead Orphans

"Cold Bones"

Shut up so I can drive, would you?" Reggie snapped as his index finger shot out, stopping just short of Malinda's nose. "I've had it with you."

Her hands flew up in resignation. "I'm just saying I'm hungry. You promised something to eat on the way to the casino." Slowly lowering her hands, Malinda continued. "You pushed me away while you were on your winning streak, and now you still don't want to stop." Her tongue dragged across her parched lips. "I'm thirsty too."

Malinda shrank into her seat, her eyes following the windshield wipers as they *whoomp-whoomped* their workman-like duty across the glass, doing their best to keep the view as clear as possible in the downpour. Realizing her heart rate was mirroring the motion of the wipers, Malinda closed her eyes and tried to slow her breathing.

"Yeah, well your fat ass could skip a few meals and still be fine." Reggie shook his head in disgust. "Should have dumped you at the casino and grabbed one of those honeys hanging all over me at the craps table." A crooked smile spread across his face. "They'd probably put out more often too." Glancing at Malinda, Reggie shook his head again, stuck with the lot he'd cast, at least for the time being. "You're just damn lucky I'm getting hungry too."

They drove in silence for several minutes, Malinda uninterested in talking to Reggie and Reggie not caring at all. As he pushed his stringy blond hair out of his eyes, Malinda eyed him. With that hair, dingy blue jeans, and faded Charlie Daniels Band t-shirt, Reggie wasn't exactly a hunk in demand. Not for the first time, Malinda wondered why she had settled for Reggie, someone who only gave her the time of day when he needed something, usually money or a blow job.

Soon, a sign along the road ahead caught Malinda's eye. "It looks like there's a pizza place up there," she whispered softly, prepared to be shouted down again.

Reggie's head bobbed. "Pizza doesn't sound half bad." He turned into the parking lot at the red, white, and green sign adorned with a slice of pizza and "Voltri's" in neon. No cars were in front of the building, and only a couple could be seen behind it. A persistent red OPEN sign blinked in the window.

They parked by the front door, hurried through the rain, and ducked into the restaurant. As soon as they stepped inside, their noses were greeted with an inebriating mixture of yeast, olive oil, and basil, which was contrasted by an equally disgusting mixture of stale beer and sweat. There were a few round tables in the center of the small room and a couple of booths along each side wall. Not asking Malinda where she wanted to sit, Reggie headed to the booth on the far side of the room, closest to the beer taps. Malinda sighed and followed him, plopping into the booth opposite him. The movement set her muffin top jiggling over the waist of her white jeans. Malinda pulled down on the hem of her vertically-striped purple and white blouse.

While they waited for a server, Malinda pushed her brown, shoulder-length hair behind an ear and looked around the restaurant. Each table was covered by a stereotypical red-and-white-checked tablecloth. A small red jar containing a lit votive candle sat in the center of each table, sandwiched between a Parmigiano Reggiano shaker on one side and salt and pepper on the other. A low wattage bulb hung in the middle of the kitchen, providing enough light to work by, but giving the interior of the restaurant a dim appearance.

Working in the kitchen was a lanky, black-haired man with the build of a breadstick. His back was to them, so Malinda couldn't see his face, but the back of the man's black pants was covered in flour. She could just see around him and watched as he worked carefully with a marble mortar and wooden pestle.

At their table appeared a young woman of the same build as the man in the kitchen, wearing a thin white gown and carrying a notepad. Long, waist-length black hair was tied in a ponytail behind her. As she reached to retrieve a pencil from behind her ear, her gown tightened against her chest, briefly flashing the darkness of an areola before it disappeared as her arm lowered. Glancing at Reggie's leering expression, Malinda knew he had seen it too.

"What can I get you to drink?" she asked with an uninterested tone.

"What do you have on tap?" Reggie asked.

Without looking, she thumbed to her left at the beer taps. "What you see there."

"Just give me a Bud. Wait, how much is it?"

"Two dollars a glass, and the servings are generous."

Reggie licked his lips. "Sounds good."

"What kind of wine do you have?" Malinda inquired.

"White or red?"

"What would you drink if it were you?" Malinda countered.

The woman perked up for the first time, pleased a customer was asking her opinion. She smiled warmly at Malinda. "I love a good red wine. We have a Ligurian red called Colli di Luni Vermentino. When I want to relax, it's what I drink."

"I will take a glass of tha—"

"How much is it?" Reggie jumped in.

"What the hell? It's not like you can't afford it," Malinda blurted, eyebrows and palms raised in confusion.

"I'm not going to spend more on you than I have to. So, I have to know how much it is."

Malinda glared across the table. "Bastard."

"Fine." He fished his wallet out of a pocket, peeled a $100 bill from the thick stack, and flung it at Malinda. "There. Consider it payment for services rendered the last six months. Find your own way home, if you don't spend it all on cheap wop wine."

Malinda snatched the bill off the table, wadding it in a clenched fist. Turning back to the server, she asked, "Can I get a whole bottle?"

The server's eyes narrowed as she stared down Reggie, the transformation quick when she turned and beamed at Malinda. "You bet, sweetie. You'll have plenty left for dinner too. I'll put yours on a separate tab. I'm Chiara. Let me know if you need anything else." She then retreated to the kitchen to turn in their order.

Malinda glared at Reggie, who pretended not to notice. Shifting her gaze to the front window, Malinda watched through the blinds as rain pelted their car. Her eyes then moved to a well-worn sign above the window, which was hand-painted black on white and read "Cà delle Anime". After a couple minutes, Chiara returned with their drinks, placing them on the table.

"What does that sign mean?" Malinda asked, nodding toward it.

Their server turned to look at the sign, inhaled slowly, and held her breath as if measuring her words. "It means 'House of Souls'." She turned back to Malinda. "It means this is a sacred place of family, a tradition going back hundreds of years. Many hearts and souls were poured into the construction of this building, this business, even before we moved here. It is all my family has known, long before they immigrated." Placing menus in front of Reggie and Malinda, Chiara detoured the conversation. "The front of the menu is designed for American tastes. The back of the menu has more traditional meals, prepared like they are in Italy."

Chiara went to the kitchen, and while Reggie and Malinda were studying their menus, she nudged the chef, held out her hand, and rubbed her fingers together as if doling out money. The man nodded and continued working.

Malinda poured a glass of wine for herself and sipped in silence while Reggie drank his beer and tried hard not to make eye contact with her. She noticed Chiara moving from table to table, blowing out the candles, until the only one lit was theirs. The server also closed the blinds and turned off the signs. When she noticed Malinda watching her, Chiara shrugged and said, "We probably aren't going to get any more customers in this weather, so we're closing up. But please, you two take your time. We live in the back half of the building, so we don't need to hurry home."

With the other candles extinguished, the restaurant assumed an even darker and eerier feel. Malinda felt a slight chill ripple up her back but ignored it and studied the menu.

"What are you going to get?" Reggie asked.

"Oh yeah, now you're talking to me," Malinda spat.

Reggie gave her a dirty look. "Just curious. I'm thinking about pizza. Ever since I saw the sign out front, I've been wanting it. Something with lots of pepperoni and cheese. As long as it's a sloppy mess, that's all I care about."

"I thought it would be nice to try something more traditional," Malinda mused softly.

"You can have that old school shit. I'm going with what I know and love."

Malinda dismissed him with a wave and studied the back of the menu. Most of the items were unfamiliar. Corzetti. Farinata. Pansotti. Burrida. Tomaxelle. Capponada. There, focaccia. She remembered seeing it on the Food Network. Giada What's-her-name made it.

Returning to their table, Chiara stood patiently with her notepad. "I just want a pepperoni pizza," Reggie announced. "Extra cheese. Might as well make it a large. I can take the leftovers to work tomorrow." He casually tossed the menu in Chiara's direction, where it slid off the table and onto the floor. She made no effort to pick it up.

"And you, sweetie?" the server asked Malinda.

"If you were ordering at a restaurant in Italy, what would you get?"

The corners of Chiara's mouth lifted higher. She liked this girl more every moment. "Probably farinata or panissa to start with. Both are made with chickpea flour and are delicious. Are you wanting something light or filling for dinner?"

Malinda thought for a bit. "Not anything heavy. It's been a long day, and it's close to bedtime. I'll be up all night if I eat too much."

Chiara nodded in understanding. "I get that. Maybe some focaccia then. We could top it with olives, tomatoes, maybe some pine nuts. It's very light, but so good when it's fresh out of the oven."

"I'll have the focaccia then," Malinda decided, giving Chiara a thumb's up. "With the farinata too." Their server wrote the order on her notepad, retrieved the menu from the floor, and left to turn in their order.

"What's with all the fancy food? Come into some money, and you need to spend it right away?" Reggie barbed. "You've always been high maintenance."

He received only a shrug in return, as Malinda was finally enjoying herself, despite her company. She closed her eyes and swayed to the song playing over the house music. Something about the moon hitting someone's eye and a pizza pie. She had heard it before but couldn't remember where.

Chiara soon came back with a plate containing a pancake topped with a green spread. "Farinata topped with fresh pesto Genovese. Papa was making it as you came in. I hope you like it."

Leaning over the plate, Malinda inhaled deeply. The aroma was intoxicating. Basil, Parmigiano Reggiano, olive oil, and pine nuts fought each other to be the most enticing scent. She lifted a slice and took a tentative bite. A moan rolled from her throat. This was easily some of the best food she'd ever had.

"Can I have some too?" Reggie asked, his voice uncommonly tender.

"Hell no. I'm paying for my meal, I get to eat it. Not my fault you didn't get an appetizer."

Reggie leaned back and crossed his arms. "Bitch."

"Maybe, but at least I'm finally my own bitch." She took another bite, relishing the magnificent blend of flavors.

Malinda had just finished her farinata when Chiara and the man from the kitchen appeared beside their table, each carrying a platter of food. She leaned back and blinked several times when she saw the chef's face. It was long and lean like the rest of his frame. Creases in his face showed he was not in the habit of smiling. A long scar ran along the side of his too-long nose and under his left eye. As pleasant and beautiful as Chiara was, her father was the opposite.

"Pizza for you," Chiara said as she slid the platter in front of Reggie. The thin crust was browned lightly, and an occasional pepperoni peeked from under the heavy blanket of mozzarella.

"And for the lady," said the chef, "Focaccia di Voltri. Seasoned with olive oil, olives, onions, tomatoes, and just a touch of sea salt. The recipe goes back longer than anyone in our family can remember." He smiled without effect, the emotion reaching no higher than his cheeks. "May we join you while you eat?"

Malinda loved the idea and slid toward the wall. She expected Chiara to sit next to her, so she was surprised when the chef scooted in beside her. Reggie realized Chiara would sit next to him, and he grinned and ogled her chest while he moved.

"I am Niccolo," the chef said, placing his palm against his chest. "And this is Gattina," he added while gesturing to Chiara.

The server laughed and blushed. "They know my name, Papa." Turning her attention to Malinda, she clarified. "Gattina just means kitten. It is a term of endearment for a daughter." She winked at her father.

"I am glad to see you chose the focaccia, young lady," Niccolo said. "Pizza is not very old in Italy. Here in America, Italian restaurants use tomatoes on everything. But long ago, we had no tomatoes. And when they first came to Italy, many people believed they were poisonous." He gestured to Malinda's platter. "Before pizza became popular, everything was served on focaccia as you have in front of you. Different regions, different toppings. But only focaccia, not pizza crust as you know it."

Chiara pointed to Reggie's pizza. "And don't even get Papa started on pepperoni."

"*Mannaggia*," Niccolo exclaimed. "In Italy, peperone means pepper. What you have on your pizza would be called salami, if I had to pick a term you know."

Finally, the two gestured for their guests to eat, and while they did so, Reggie and Malinda were regaled with stories of the Liguria region of Italy and their hosts' home just outside Genoa. Malinda absorbed it all, enraptured, but Reggie mostly ate, sighed, and regularly checked his watch.

When they had finished eating, Chiara cleared the dishes then reclaimed her spot beside Reggie. She moved close, ensuring her arm and leg touched his.

"Now, Reggie, I can tell by the look in your eye you are a gambling man," Niccolo said softly. Reggie agreed tentatively, unsure how the chef knew his name.

"Good, good. Gambling goes back a long time in Italy, back to the Romans. Dice in particular." He leaned forward and held Reggie's gaze. "Do you like dice games?"

"Depends on if the odds are in my favor. But I've had a good stroke of luck today. What's your game?"

Niccolo sat back and pulled a pair of dice from his pocket, tossing them on the table. As he did so, Malinda realized the candle at their table was the only light in the restaurant. She could not even see any passing cars between the blinds.

"Please, check them out," the chef instructed. Reggie lifted a die, examined it, then the other. He tossed them several times, at different angles, trying to find a pattern in them. Satisfied there was none, he placed the dice on the table.

"Talk to me," Reggie instructed.

"It's simple. You roll the dice. Whatever they add up to, that's your number. You decide if the next roll will be higher or lower and win if you are right."

Reggie studied the man. "And the bet?"

"One hundred dollars a roll. If the game pleases you, we can increase the bets as we go."

Thinking back on his luck earlier that evening, Reggie liked his odds. He had been so hot, the casino eventually shut down the craps table. He had several thousand dollars in his wallet and even more in his pockets. "Let's do this."

Reggie scooped the dice, studied Niccolo briefly, then rolled. Four. "Easy," he announced. "Higher." The next roll was an eleven.

"Well done, my friend." Niccolo dug five twenties from his pocket and placed them in front of Reggie. "Again?" the chef prompted.

"Absolutely. I'm up." Reggie rolled again. Ten. "Lower." His next roll was a three. Niccolo smiled and placed more bills in front of Reggie. He laughed and winked at Malinda, who was bored with the events and just sipped her wine.

Reggie won four more times, prompting Chiara to retrieve cash from the register to pay his winnings. He eyed the stack of cash in front of him, and patted it lightly, feeling the roughness of the bills against his palm.

"You seem to be doing well, my friend. Are you willing to up the stakes?" Niccolo said to Reggie, showing his emotionless smile. When Reggie nodded in return, the chef added, "A thousand a roll."

Reggie laughed. "You're having to raid your register as it is. You can't keep losing."

Chiara leaned closer to Reggie and whispered, "If we run out of money, you can have me. One night for every time we lose." She punctuated the offer with a caress on the inside of Reggie's thigh. He flushed but made no move to stop her.

"And if I lose? That could burn through my cash pretty fast."

"No money. You go home with no less cash than what you have now, plus anything you win." Niccolo leaned toward Reggie. "If we win, you leave part of yourself here." Reggie felt his will melt away as he drowned in his host's eyes. For her part, Chiara moved her caresses higher, making it very clear what Reggie stood to gain.

Reggie glanced at Malinda, then to Chiara. As he looked at her, she leaned forward and gave him a brief kiss. The faint fragrance of roses lingered after their lips parted. Malinda watched the events with amusement. Past the breaking point with Reggie, she was curious to see what would happen next.

Without looking away from Chiara, Reggie found himself saying, "Deal."

Niccolo went to the kitchen, returning with a cleaver. Reggie blanched at the sight of the blade, but his head, both for that matter, could only think of Chiara.

The chef gathered the dice and closed his fist around them. A chilling breeze swept over them, making the lone candle flicker. Malinda rubbed her bare arms, finding the hair on them standing up. Something wasn't right. She felt a strong compulsion to flee but had to see what happened next.

Niccolo offered the dice to Reggie. "Your roll."

Reggie took the dice, which were frigid against the palm of his hand. He looked from Chiara to Niccolo to Malinda, then back at Chiara. Then he rolled. Two. Reggie let out an audible sigh. Higher. He grabbed the cold dice from the table and rolled them in the same motion. Five.

"Very good, my friend." Niccolo disappeared to an office behind the kitchen and reappeared with a small stack of bills bound together by a leather tie. As the chef fanned through the stack, Reggie estimated in his head. *There can't be more than a few hundred dollars there*, he thought. It was his now, plus some time with Chiara. His eyes found hers, and she kissed him again, filling his mind with all the things he would do to her tonight.

"Another time?" Niccolo asked.

Reggie agreed, grabbed the dice, and rolled. Ten. "Lower", he guessed. Then another roll, which produced a four. Every roll got him more aroused and more anxious to roll again. He began rolling and guessing in quick succession, never noticing the dice remained ice cold despite the warmth of his hand.

Nine. Lower. Five.

Four. Higher. Six.

Three. Higher. Nine.

Ten. Lower. Eleven.

Reggie blinked several times at the dice on the table. They were very clearly a five and six, where the previous roll had been two fives. Uncertainty dominated his face as he looked at Niccolo.

"Which hand do you write with?" the chef asked.

"Right," his guest answered. Niccolo gestured for Reggie's left hand, which Reggie gave with trepidation. The chef gently folded Reggie's fingers into a fist except for his pinkie. Holding Reggie's hand down tightly, Niccolo put the tip of the cleaver on the opposite side of the extended finger, rocking the cleaver back and forth in a mesmerizing motion. Reggie's mind screamed for him to pull his hand away, but his body refused to listen.

The cleaver fell abruptly, making a sound reminding Malinda of her mother chopping carrots. As the blade severed the first joint of Reggie's pinkie, blood spattered onto Malinda's arm. She dabbed at it absently with her napkin then lowered her gaze at Reggie. "Roll again," she said while grinning. "I like this game."

Reggie stared at her in confusion. He'd never seen this fire in her eyes, and he didn't like it. Yet he found himself grabbing the dice again with his good hand. Chiara watched him with her slightly parted lips, which reinforced his desire to continue, despite the intense throbbing pain he felt.

He rolled again. Six. Reggie gulped while deciding how to bet. Soon he blurted "Higher". Another roll. Two.

"Snake eyes, my friend," Niccolo chuckled, the laughter and smile finally reaching his eyes. Without hesitation, the chef clamped down on Reggie's hand and severed the next knuckle from his bloody finger.

Feeling woozy, Reggie eyed the spreading pool of blood, which now surrounded the dice. Had his luck changed? Or was this just a speed bump in an otherwise fabulous day? He wanted to stop. He needed to stop.

Detached from his own actions, he watched his good hand pluck the dice from the table, wiping the blood from them onto his shirt. He clutched them tightly, but they were just as icy as before. Taking a deep breath, he prepared to roll.

"Wait," Niccolo commanded. "One final roll. For all the marbles, so to speak." Reggie waited, the cold from the dice burning his hand, before nodding assent. "You win, you keep Chiara forever. We win, she keeps you forever."

Reggie held Chiara's gaze, his aching for her sharper than the pain he felt. His hand throbbed, but it was dulled by his lust. *Either way, I get her*, he thought. He glanced at Malinda, who just gestured for him to roll and be done with it.

Leaning forward, Reggie gave Chiara a long kiss, and she reciprocated with enthusiasm. His face showing smug confidence, Reggie rolled the dice. Three. "Hot damn, higher," Reggie exclaimed and rolled again. The dice stopped inside the pool of blood, two dark eyes staring up at him.

Reggie didn't care what the dice showed. He had his prize. Looking at Chiara, he smirked. "Looks like you get to have me."

"Indeed I do, lover." Chiara pursed her lips, and as Reggie leaned in for a kiss, she snatched the cleaver from the table and swung it across the front of his throat. Reggie's lecherous smile faded, replaced by a crimson one a few inches lower.

Malinda raised her eyebrows and smiled. "Damn" was all she could manage.

Blood seeped from the wound, joined soon by bubbles as Reggie fought to find his breath. He clutched his throat, which only forced the gaping wound wider. He struggled for a few moments before collapsing back in the booth. Before Malinda's eyes, he began melting away, clothes and all, like butter in a hot skillet. As the shrinking mass that used to be her boyfriend slipped under the table, Malinda lifted her feet to rest against the table pedestal. These were new Nikes after all. Had she looked under the table, Malinda would have seen nothing but Reggie's cash.

Not long after Malinda's ex-boyfriend vanished, a wisp of red smoke rose from the floor and drifted toward the wall. As the smoke reached the wall, it was absorbed, and a crack in the plaster disappeared.

Malinda stared at Chiara and Niccolo for a moment. "Damn" was all she could muster again. When they only stared back, she asked, "Check please?"

"Don't worry, pretty lady," Niccolo intoned. "Tonight's dinner is—" He glanced at the recently repaired wall. "—on the house." He retrieved the cleaver from his daughter and began cleaning it on a linen napkin.

Malinda thanked him and began scooting toward the outside of the booth, but the chef wouldn't budge. Her eyes found his, willing him to move. "Excuse me?" she added. Niccolo only smiled back.

"Pretty lady, you deserved someone better than him. But tonight, you were just in the wrong car," he whispered, then the blade fell.

Author Notes

This was a story I wrote for a submission call for pizza-themed horror stories. I actually stewed on the idea while waiting for my father-in-law to get out of surgery, and the first thing I wanted to look for was some lore or legends of Italy.

One I ran across was an inn called Casa delle Anime, abbreviated Ca' delle Anime, the so-called House of Souls near Voltri in the Liguria region of Italy. In the Middle Ages, the inn sat on a frequently-traveled path, and naturally many weary travelers would stop there.

However, some of them were never heard from again, especially wealthy ones. But unlike my story, where the victims encountered death by blade, the unfortunate travelers at Casa delle Anime would be placed in a special room where the ceiling would be slowly lowered while they slept, crushing them. There are even rumors the disposed-of travelers ended up on the dinner table for future guests.

Obviously, in my story the travelers also happen to have a lot of money in hand, stopped for a meal, and pay the price for it. There was nothing in the Casa delle Anime story about the death of the travelers healing the house. It just sounded like an interesting addition on my part.

There are tidbits in this story that were fun researching, especially the food and wine of the region. Of course, dice games are part of almost all cultures including ancient Romans, so it made sense to use that to draw in a gambling-obsessed Reggie. Add in Malinda, who had finally reached her breaking point with him, and a beautiful server who promised him a good time, and he never stood a chance.

And Malinda? She just waited one day too long to break free from Reggie.

"Conchita"

The crash from the shattering plate echoed through the resort's dining area, and silence rippled through the patrons before they returned to their conversations. A five-year-old girl picked up pieces of the plate she had dropped, tears welling in the corners of her eyes.

"*No no, niña, esta bien,*" a lanky man sporting a chef's coat and floppy toque consoled her. "*Esta bien.*"

He looked about for a parent, spotting a portly man stalking toward them, his face etched with a scowl and furrowed brow. The man carried a plate piled high with seafood and fruit, the other hand rapidly opening and closing in a fist. As he approached, his mouth and jaw worked, the mole at the tip of his mustache jerking angrily with each motion.

Without a word, he snatched the pieces of the plate from the girl's hands, thrusting them at the chef. He grabbed the little girl's arm and turned quickly, pulling her behind as he stormed to their table.

At the table, he put down his plate with a clatter, lifted the girl, and dropped her into the chair beside his. As she fell into her chair, the girl's pink t-shirt pulled up under her armpits, and she wiggled to pull it back down before anyone could see. Just as he got settled, a server appeared. She looked from the man to the girl and back, a questioning look on her face.

"*Mojito,*" he spat at the server while tapping his empty glass. The server waited to see if the man would order anything for the girl, but when he remained silent, she nodded and left to get his drink.

The little girl peeked from behind the curtain of black hair in her face, her eyes shifting from his plate of food to the empty spot in front of her. She shifted in her chair so she was sitting on her heels and drank some water. It didn't help with the pangs in her stomach, so she finished the glass. Still didn't help.

The girl felt bad for dropping the plate. All she had wanted to do was get food without her father's help, something he allowed on occasion, but she had been careless. Hopefully the resort wouldn't make them pay for the plate.

"*Tengo hambre, papá,*" she said to her father as she pressed her hand against her stomach. He grunted in return and tossed a piece of pineapple onto her placemat. She picked up the fruit and slowly nibbled on it, resisting the urge to wolf it down. When she got to the core, it was much harder, but she chewed it until she could finally swallow it.

The server returned and refilled their water glasses. The man tapped his empty drink and slurred "*uno mas*". A couple minutes later, he had a fresh cocktail in front of him.

Looking to the top of the soaring roof of the dining area, the girl saw a peacock perched on a rafter, its stunning feathers of blue and green draped behind it. Those feathers seemed to dance and sway with the island music playing throughout the restaurant. The bird reminded her of the peacocks she had seen with Princess Jasmine in a Disney movie. They were beautiful, and not only that, they could fly, as the bird perched on the high rafter showed.

She wondered what it would be like to be able to fly. Not on a magic carpet like Jasmine and Ali, but like a bird, soaring among the clouds, far above everyone, flying high and free.

Eyes closed, imagining herself swooping among the palm trees, the little girl flapped her arms to make the illusion as real as possible. This earned a sharp slap on the arm from her father. Her eyes shot open, and she grabbed her arm, which was already turning an angry red, the fire from the strike making her arm hot to the touch.

An older couple at a nearby table frowned at her father, shook their heads, then returned to their meals, mumbling something in a language the girl couldn't understand. The man had chicken strips and mango on his plate, and the little girl wished she was at their table. She was certain they would take care of her, feed her, smother her with hugs and kisses.

The girl rubbed the mark on her arm, wondering if a dark bruise would replace the red. If so, it would match the many marks covering her body, from a faint yellow to a deep purple. On her chest, her back, and between her legs.

A piece of melon landed in front of the girl. She eyed her father, then picked it up and ate it slowly. Any time he hurt her, he was always kind to her soon after. Never with words, but with actions, such as the gifted fruit. It was how she knew he loved her.

Several times this year, the two had made the trip from Santo Domingo to the resort in Bávaro, just to get away from the hustle and bustle of the capital. Each time, her father became more interested in food and drink and less interested in her. But the little girl loved the trips, especially the stunning beach, palm trees, and beautiful peacocks, flamingos, egrets, and other birds wandering the resort. She had even seen some lizards and turtles.

When her father's plate was empty, and he had polished off two more cocktails, he rose without a word and stumbled toward the exit. The girl scrambled down from her chair and chased after him. She heard a soft *"adios"* and turned to find the server waving at her. The girl offered a weak smile for the woman then hurried after her father.

She trailed behind him like an obedient pet, careful to stay close but remain behind him. It wouldn't do any good to hold his hand, no matter how much she wanted to, because it wasn't something her *papá* did. So she just followed him around the pool as he headed toward the beach.

Just as they reached the sand, he stopped at a palapa bar, and they received a friendly *"¿Qué lo que?"* and grin from the bartender. Her father pointed at a bottle of Brugal Añejo rum on a shelf behind the man. *"Ron, por favor,"* he mumbled.

The bartender grabbed the new bottle, opened it, and started to pour some into a plastic cup. *"No no no,"* her father grumbled, grabbing the bottle and dropping a thousand peso bill on the counter. He stalked off without waiting for his daughter.

She looked up at the bartender, a blank expression on her face as she rubbed her belly. The man nodded slowly, grabbed an orange, and sliced it. He dropped the pieces into a plastic cup and handed it down to her. "*Una naranja, niña linda.*" Accepting the gift without a word, she hurried after her father.

It was dark, so it was hard for the girl to find him. A lounge chair had been dragged toward the water, and there she found her father, straddling the chair and drinking greedily from his bottle. She sat in the sand a few feet away and ate her orange in silence. When she was done, the girl put the cup down, twisting it back and forth to make an impromptu cup holder in the sand.

The repetitive sound of the surf was soothing to the girl, and she closed her eyes, blocking out all sounds except for the water and a soft drift of laughter from far away. Aromas of salt and seaweed, tempered by the acrid odor of the rum, filled her nostrils.

She thought not of Jasmine now, but Ariel. The girl had always wanted to learn to swim, but it wasn't something her *papá* had ever taught her. Only faint memories of her mother remained, disappearing from their lives some time ago, although she had no concept of how long.

Her parents had gotten into a heated argument, and they disappeared to their bedroom, the door slamming behind them. Later, her father had turned off the TV in the middle of the girl's favorite movie and told her to go to bed, which she did. She hadn't seen her mother since.

A deep rumble reached the girl's ears, and she looked up at her father, finding him on his side in the lounge chair, empty bottle of rum in the sand beside him. His snoring stopped briefly as he changed sides, turning his back to her. Soon the racket continued.

The girl spread her feet and used her hands to smooth a patch in the sand in front of her. In her makeshift tablet, she wrote a "C". Beside it, she drew an "O". Pondering for a minute, the girl chewed on her lip and stared at her writing, illuminated by the full moon.

There was more to write, but she didn't know it yet. So below the original letters, she wrote two more identical ones. And below those, two more.

"*Hola, chiquita,*" came a soft voice beside her. The girl looked up and found their server squatting beside her. The woman pointed to the writing. "*¿Tu nombre?*"

Looking at the writing then back to the woman, the girl formed her hand in a "C" and pointed to the moon. "*La luna.*" Then she made an "O" with both hands. "*Tambien la luna.*"

"*Ah, si,*" the woman replied, and she stroked the girl's hair. "*Me llamo Adriana,*" she added, pointing to her name tag. "*¿Y tu?*"

The girl hovered her finger beside the "O" closest to her in the sand, hesitated, then looked back to Adriana. "*Conchita.*"

"*¡Ah, que bella!*" the server cooed. She leaned forward and completed Conchita's name on each line in the sand. "*Conchita,*" she pronounced and smiled.

"*Gracias,*" the girl answered without looking up.

Andriana eyed the man passed out on the nearby lounge chair. "*¿Tu papá?*" Conchita nodded. "*¿Dónde está tu mamá?*" Adriana asked while looking around. "*¿Mamá?*"

Conchita said nothing, erasing the bottom two rows of her name in the sand. With meticulous detail she added two rows identical to the first, smiling up at Adriana. The woman returned the joy and clapped softly.

A loud ruckus reached the two, and when they looked back toward the resort, two men were throwing punches at each other, a woman behind each one yelling in English. Adriana placed a quick kiss on the top of the girl's head, said "*Un momento, chiquita,*" then hurried off toward the fight.

When the woman was gone, Conchita returned her attention to the writing in the sand. Again she erased the bottom two lines and wrote her name twice. Then, taking a deep breath, she erased all three lines. After scratching her cheek for a moment, she correctly wrote her name in neat block letters.

Pleased with herself, the girl looked to her father, but he still had his back turned to her. Adriana was still trying, along with a couple co-workers, to de-escalate the scuffle.

Turning her attention to the water, Conchita watched the waves roll in, the sound soothing. While she didn't like how the splashing salt water stung her nose and throat when her *mamá* had carried her into the water, she loved the aroma of the salt air, and she loved the feel of sand against her skin.

Her thoughts returned again to Ariel. How amazing it must be to be a mermaid and swim away from everything, your trusty but talkative sidekick at your side. Conchita lost interest in the movie whenever Ariel was on land. But when she was in the sea? Yes, that's when she paid the most attention.

As she watched the waves, Conchita saw a flash of blue, green, and silver in the waves, followed by a brief glimpse of red. It was her! The girl was certain of it. She rose and tried to focus on the spot in the surf where she'd seen the mermaid.

Just as Conchita thought it had been a mistake, she caught another glimpse of sparkling color. She was certain Ariel was there, waving to her. Conchita waved back and took a couple steps toward the surf, excitement broadening the smile across her face. She jumped up and down, clapped her hands quickly, and took a few more steps.

When she stopped, the water came forward just enough to get her wet from the ankles down. Conchita took a hesitant step back, waited for the water to recede, then moved forward even more. This time, when the waves came in, she got wet up to her knees, the splashing water reaching the bottom of her pink shorts and sprinkling droplets of water across her shirt.

From far behind the girl came a loud shout, "*¡Conchita! ¡Conchita, no!*"

When the girl heard her name, she glanced out to the water, certain she was being called. Sure enough, just beyond a breaking wave, she could see the mermaid, waving and gesturing for Conchita to join her. The girl smiled and took several steps toward her favorite character.

As the waves came in again, the water was up to Conchita's waist, striking her hard enough to make her wobble. And when the waves returned home, the undertow seized the little girl's ankles and took her with it.

Conchita suddenly found herself underwater, her eyes, nose, and mouth stinging from the salt, her lungs filling with water and sand. She swung her arms and spun around, one hand briefly grabbing a handful of sand, the other only air.

For a brief moment, she found herself on her knees, head barely above water, then a wave much taller than her struck her back, knocking her down, filling her mouth with sand and surf. As she fell and kicked, one pink shoe flew from her foot and landed on the beach.

A few seconds later, the water returned, claiming the shoe for an owner who no longer needed it. Conchita was finally free to swim with the mermaids.

Author Notes

Back in early 2020, just before the pandemic broke loose, My Gorgeous Bride and I went to the Punta Cana/Bávaro region of the Dominican Republic to celebrate her birthday. We stayed at an all-inclusive resort and, unrelated to this story, became totally obsessed with the country and its beaches.

One day, when we were in the buffet area for dinner, I heard a crash and saw a little girl had dropped her plate of food, which she had been filling herself. She was probably five or six, if I had to guess. Soon, a man, who I presumed was her father, came up and started scolding her in Spanish, then he led her off to their table.

In the real world, he ended up getting some food for her while she waited at the table. But the happenings made me wonder, what if he wasn't such a good, loving dad? What if he was flat out neglectful? What would their backstory have been? And what could go wrong from that?

This story developed from that experience when I saw a submission call for stories based in various countries around the world. Obviously it wasn't selected, but I still really liked it, so I filed it away for future submissions.

When I put this story in front of my beta readers, a couple were afraid this could be perceived as derogatory toward Dominicans. Obviously, there are good and bad people in all cultures and countries. But I want to explicitly say that all the Dominicans I have ever interacted with were amazingly kind and loving, and by all accounts, great parents.

Plus, as I pointed out to those readers, there are a lot of Spanish-speaking expats who live in and tourists who visit the Dominican Republic, not just locals. The point is obviously that there are some terrible dads everywhere. And sometimes their progeny pay the price.

"Tough Love"

Thomas moved the fish around his mouth with his tongue, finally separating the annoying bone from the meat and spitting the bone into the sand beside him. Using the thin strip of metal he had fashioned into an impromptu spatula and knife, Thomas flipped the fish he was cooking. A wider piece of metal served as both griddle and plate, which was laid across the open campfire.

"Roxy would have loved this," he found himself saying to the emptiness. His fiancée fancied herself a pescatarian, so this meal, accompanied by some fresh greens, would have been right up her alley.

After determining the fish was cooked on both sides, Thomas removed the griddle from the flame and set it aside. He didn't bother to put out the campfire. It's not like there was much of anything to set aflame, especially since he was surrounded by water. What, burn down a few trees? Who gives a damn? It would just seal his fate that much quicker when he couldn't start a fire anymore.

Thomas rose and wandered down the beach to the few pieces of plane wreckage he had managed to drag ashore. When the plane went down several hundred yards out, he was lucky to have survived the impact. His collegiate swimming scholarship had finally paid off, even if his degree in kinesiology hadn't. He had to drag Roxy to the shore with him following the crash, but he wasn't about to let her go down with the wreckage. No other survivors had made it to shore.

He moved around the salvaged parts for the umpteenth time today, not sure what he was looking for. Wading into the surf, Thomas swam for a while, looking for crabs like those he had seen scuttling across the sand earlier in the day. Not having any luck, he returned to shore and paced slowly along the beach, letting the sun and light breeze dry him off. He hated sand and didn't want it stuck all over his wet body.

Surviving on seafood wasn't high on Thomas's priority list. Sure, lobster was always good when slathered in butter, but only if it was accompanied by a healthy-sized ribeye. Medium rare, maybe even a little rare. Heaven. Pure heaven.

Thomas sighed heavily and plopped down next to his meal, spraying sand onto the fish. Cursing, he picked up the plate then picked and flicked sand off the fish until it was clean to his satisfaction. Even then, his first bite had a gritty crunch to it. Just as he was about to take another bite, a foot-wide crab appeared from the surf in front of him, paused for a moment, then disappeared back into the water.

Cursing again, Thomas flung his plate like a Frisbee, the plate arcing in one direction while the fish flew in another. He sat, debating with himself what he should do next, then got up and paced the shoreline again. When he reached the salvaged wreckage, his anger and frustration building, he grabbed pieces indiscriminately and began tossing them back toward the water. Most didn't make it that far, so he picked them up again and made sure they were in the water, even though they were quickly uncovered and covered again by the surf.

"Fuck it," he yelled again to an audience of none and stalked back toward the campfire. Tracking down his plate, he rinsed it off in the surf and placed it back on the campfire to heat again, waiting until water flicked from his fingertips immediately turned to steam on the metal surface.

Grabbing the knife from the sand and wiping it on his still-wet cargo shorts, Thomas walked calmly to the nearest tree, where Roxy's remains hung by her ankles. Using the knife, he sawed a large, jagged chunk of flesh from her thigh, then returned to the campfire and tossed his meal onto the sizzling griddle.

Squatting next to the fire, Thomas deeply inhaled the intoxicating aroma. Finally. Red meat.

Author Notes

This story was actually one that just came to me, rather than being the product of a submission call. At one point, I heard the phrase "tender lover" and I pondered, "What if that were literal?"

Around that time I heard someone talking about the movie "Castaway" with Tom Hanks, and that struck me as a good setting for such a story. And away I went.

"It's Always the Quiet Ones"

Ethel jerked her thumb at the man sitting behind her. "That's the fella you want. Best carpet muncher in the whole place."

Leaning to their left in synch, Louise and Sue eyed him with skepticism, then leaned back at the same time.

Sue stuck her finger in Ethel's face. "Bullshit. Old fart can barely sit up straight at the table. No way he could rock my world like that."

All three pretended to focus on their Yahtzee game as a nurse walked by, waiting until she was out of earshot to continue. Louise rolled the dice for the final time in her move and wrote down her score.

Ethel raised her hands in defense. "I'm just tellin' ya what I've heard. Lots o' girls here say Frankie gave 'em the best eatin' they ever had. Even a couple o' the nurses say so. An' they're young'uns an' not so desperate."

The object of their attention got up from his spot at the table and slowly made his way down the hallway to his room, leaning heavily on his cane the whole way. "Bullshit," Sue repeated. "He moves like old people fuck. So to speak. I don't believe you."

Another nurse came by, asking the ladies how they were, moving on once she was assured they were well. Ethel had to admit this nursing home wasn't too bad, considering how much she hated the idea when she came here six years ago. But she had grown to love the place, even more so once the ladies in her present company joined her there. They had become fast friends and been almost inseparable since.

"He's probably one who'll want a suck off once he's done, and it'll take forever if he can't keep wood," Sue pondered out loud.

"Naw," Ethel assured her, "I heard he don't expect nothin' in return. Just enjoys doin' his job, then he goes. Don't even need any of that cuddlin' crap."

"I got ninety-nine problems, but a dick ain't one!" Sue cackled at her own humor, slapping her knee as the other two looked on with bewilderment.

"Aw, come on, you can't tell me you don't know any Jay-Z, girls. That's even some of his old shit." Her friends continued to regard Sue with the same expressions.

Louise shook her head, rose, circled to her left around the table, then headed down the hallway back toward her room. The other two watched her go and decided to end their game. Soon, they followed Louise down the hallway, catching up with her just as she arrived at her room.

"I'm a-tellin' ya, Sue, it's worth checkin' out. A girl don't get the chance to make wet spots and bad words very often."

"Yeah, like you can even make wet spots anymore, Ethel."

Louise settled into her recliner, grabbed the TV remote, and channel surfed until she found a NASCAR race. She smiled and was soon absorbed in it.

"Thing is," Sue continued, "I hear he don't do it for free. He wants somethin' in return. A gift. But it's gotta be somethin' different. Somethin' unique. Kinda like a trophy case he's buildin', but nobody knows what each one is for except the one who gave it to him."

"Yeah, but what? What kind of shit has he gotten before?"

Scratching her chin, Ethel shrugged. "All I know is Marie said she got him some shrunken head from Africa or somethin'. And that fat bitch nurse that loves givin' enemas so much was supposed to have gotten him the first Spider-Man comic. So weird shit like that."

A male nurse stuck his head into Louise's room, looked around to make sure nobody had fallen or was otherwise distressed, then left without a word. "Well, Sue, I guess we're just gonna have to go down to see what all he's got so we can get some ideas. You comin', Lefty?" she said to Louise, who in return just flapped a hand at them to shoo them away, her eyes never leaving the TV.

28

The other two took off down the hallway toward Frankie's room, careful to go slowly in case the nurses would think they were up to something. Which they were, of course.

Arriving at Frankie's room, Ethel and Sue positioned themselves on either side of the door, then leaned in slightly so they could see his side of the room. He had two bookshelves lined with all manner of oddities: the aforementioned shrunken head, an old rotary telephone, a beat-up alto saxophone, a folded Nazi flag, a Mercedes Benz hood ornament, and countless other items.

Sue leaned back against the wall. "We're fucked. None of us has anything other than granny panties and Depends to our name. No way we can find something original and unique like what he's already got."

Her partner in crime wasn't paying any attention, as she was looking beyond Frankie's stash, out his window to the Fed Ex truck making a delivery across the street. "Girl, I think I got us a plan."

The next day, the three ladies were sitting in the rocking chairs outside the front door of the nursing home, pretending to enjoy the fresh air while their attending nurse, who was barely out of high school, focused intently on her iPhone. They rocked slowly, passing time, stopping in unison when the Fed Ex truck pulled in front of the home across the street. The driver got out carrying a package and fast walked to the front door, quickly pushing the doorbell. As expected, the mid-forties housewife answered the door, wearing nothing but a short wrap that barely covered her naughty bits, and the two disappeared inside.

Sue glanced at her watch to note the time, and the girls started rocking again. At just under ten minutes later, the young man exited the house, grinning from ear to ear and still carrying the same package, got into his truck, and left. The three looked at each other and smiled, their plan developing quickly. For the next two days, the three of them repeated their routine while the driver and housewife repeated theirs.

"I'm a-tellin' you, this will work. That truck will have all kinds o' shit in it we can pick from for Frankie. Each of us can get somethin' we think will be interestin', and we can each get our turn with him cleanin' our cooches." Ethel was the mastermind who started this, and there was no way she was letting it go now.

"You know," Sue added, "Tomorrow is pork chop day. They only puree that shit for those who don't have good jaw teeth anymore. We can snatch the steak knives to use for opening packages. I think it will work."

Louise nodded while walking in circles to her left around Sue's half of her room. The lady in the other half of the room was in late stages of dementia and completely unaware of her surroundings, occasionally yelling "Fuck!" at the top of her lungs for no apparent reason.

Ethel watched Louise making her laps, as her plan continued to develop. "We know the code to get out, so that ain't no problem. We gotta distract the nurses so they don't see us go. So we gotta figure that out. Or just hope there's a time the nursin' station is empty. But it's gotta happen at the right time, or we're screwed."

"Fuck!" The three of them jumped as Sue's roomie let out her regular exclamation.

"I really hate that bitch, you know?" Sue shook her head, paused, then looked over her readers at Ethel. "Girl, I think I know what we need to do."

Friday was the big day, as the girls hatched out their plans. Sue was the fastest of them, so she was The Chosen One. Plus, this part was her idea and up to her to pull off. The other two waited at the corner of the hallway nearest the nursing station, the front door only twenty feet to their right.

Creeping to her roomie's bed, Sue pulled one of the pillows from below the woman's head. Looking at the eyes staring blankly at the ceiling, Sue clinched the pillow several times with her hands, then leaned forward and pushed the pillow down with all her strength, covering the old lady's face.

Clawed hands reached up and weakly pulled at the pillow. A muffled "Fuh! Fuh! Fuh!" came from under the pillow, the hands pulling more frantically but more weakly at the pillow, until they slowly dropped on either side of the bed. Sue lifted the old lady's head, placed the pillow under her head, and reverently closed her eyes.

She turned to alert a nurse, only then realizing she'd left the door open the whole time. Damn lucky, she was. Sticking her head out the door, Sue yelled as loud as she could, "Nurse! Help! I think Miss Eleanor is dead!"

Nurses quickly vacated their station, and Sue took the opportunity to shuffle past them to her waiting friends. Ethel and Sue rounded the corner toward the front door, leaving Louise behind as she turned to her left until she'd gone a full 270 degrees to catch up with them. Shaking her head, Ethel grinned at her eccentric friend. "Ol' Left Turn Louise. Shoulda been a NASCAR driver."

The three of them reached the door, entered the code, and scooted outside, quickly moving to the other side of a tall bush. They pressed as closely together as they could, hoping nobody had noticed their escape. After a couple minutes had passed, they relaxed and waited for their treasure chest to arrive.

"Shit. Shit shit shit shit shit."

Louise and Sue eyed Ethel with curiosity. "I forgot the steak knives. They're under my mattress, where I put them after lunch."

"Shit," Sue echoed in sympathy. Louise just nodded, her brows furrowed.

Before they could develop an alternate plan, the Fed Ex truck came rumbling down the road. "If we don't do it now, we gotta wait until Monday to try again," Ethel said. "Ain't none of us even sure we won't be takin' a dirt nap by then."

The other two nodded and watched as the delivery truck parked across the street. As planned, they started moving toward it as soon as it stopped, knowing the driver would get out on his side and never see them approaching. Sure enough, he did just that, hopping down from his perch, package in hand, and practically running to the front door.

The three ladies reached the truck and pressed their backs against it, staying motionless until they heard the front door open and close again. They shuffled slowly up the steps and settled into the cargo area of the truck.

"Look, a box cutter." Sue pointed at the various items hanging on the wall, including a tape gun and tape measure. "We can use that to open shit."

31

The box cutter was snatched up, and Sue began quickly cutting open boxes as Ethel and Louise dug through them. They went through quite a few packages, garnering only books, dishes, an air freshener, a box of hammers, and several other mundane items. Eventually, Ethel pulled out an electric wand vibrator. "Now this is a gift to me. Ol' bastard can't have that," she grinned.

They continued to dig through the boxes, not finding anything of use, stopping suddenly when they heard the front door open. "Shit, how long's it been, Sue?"

"I don't know, I didn't look at my watch. We just got to working on opening shit." A faint whistle grew louder as the driver approached. "Fuck. We can't let him find all this. He'll flip his shit."

The driver hopped into his seat still whistling, but stopped abruptly when he felt Sue's hand across his forehead and something cold and sharp against his neck. "Hey there, pretty boy. Nice song there. Amazing what some pussy can do for a fella's mood. Why don't you come with me into the back." As he moved to the back, his look of fear turned to bewilderment as he realized his attackers' ages were almost ten times his when combined.

"Aw, come on ladies, there's no need for this." He reached up to pull down the box cutter in Sue's hand, and Ethel, who was sitting on a nearby box, rapped him sharply in the knee cap with a hammer. "What the hell was that?" he exclaimed as he began hopping around. Sue, who was almost a foot shorter than him, struggled to keep the blade against his neck. For good measure, Ethel hit him even harder in the other knee, and he collapsed, crying and rolling around the floor of the truck.

"Well now what, you dumbfuck?" Sue asked Ethel, who shrugged with her hands, hammer still gripped tightly. Louise wasn't much help either, as she was walking in tight circles to her left, stepping over and around packages as she went.

Sue sighed. "Well, we know he can make that slut inside happy, so let's see what he can do for me." She wiggled out of her granny panties, propped each foot on a nearby box and eyed the driver. "Come here, you young stud," she coaxed, gesturing with the box cutter. "Or else."

Having learned rather abruptly how serious these ladies were, the driver tried walking on his knees toward Sue, but kept falling over from the pain. "Ethel, give this pussy some ghost turds to kneel on or something." Her friend obliged by dumping the packaging from several boxes on the floor between Sue's legs. When she was done, the driver moved cautiously toward the task ahead, his eyes never leaving it.

"Come on, I don't have all day. We're probably getting our asses thrown in jail today, so I want one last hurrah before I go, because I ain't letting no dykes go down there when I'm in the pokey." Sue eyed the driver and gestured downward again with the box cutter.

The driver began his unenviable task with no enthusiasm. Sue was was not impressed. "Boy, what are you doing? You act like you're allergic to lollipops. You got to get all up in there like you mean it." She grabbed his shoulders and pulled him closer as hard as she could. The driver pulled back. Sue pulled him closer. This tug-of-war continued until the driver collapsed motionless on the floor.

"What the fuck?" Sue asked as she leaned forward. Lifting her hands, she eyed the blood covering the box cutter and her hand, not to mention the deep gash in the side of the driver's neck. "Well, shit. Oh well, boy didn't know what he was doing anyway." She stood up, retrieved her panties, and after eying the blood stains on them, tossed them toward the back of the truck.

"Well now what?" Ethel asked her homicidal friend. "That's two today. You fixin' to off us too?"

As they stared each other down, one wielding a box cutter while the other waved a hammer, the truck lurched forward, causing them to fall. They looked up and saw Louise perched behind the wheel, her ass barely clinging to the edge of the seat as she pushed down on the accelerator with the tip of her foot.

Sue and Ethel sat quietly on the floor for a few minutes, deciding it was best they didn't know whether or not Louise was driving the truck well. They enjoyed the calm for a while, something that had been in short supply that day.

Catching a glimpse of something shiny under the driver, Sue pushed him up on one shoulder and retrieved a necklace from around his neck. After wiping the blood off on her gown, she examined it. It was a penis and balls. As she pulled down on a ring, she noticed the penis rise as if erect. She made the motion multiple times, cackling and watching the penis go up and down. "Now this is something that's different."

"Yes, it is," Ethel agreed and buried the claw end of the hammer into the base of her friend's skull. She watched as Sue fell over sideways, hands still clutching her prize. "I know my ass was gettin' killed next anyway. Now there's just one more piece of business."

Ethel worked her way forward until she had reached the driver's seat. She placed one hand on the back of the seat and one on the roof of the truck, balancing herself as she looked down at her friend. Louise looked up at her, grinned broadly, and returned her eyes to the road. Ethel was impressed with how well her friend was maneuvering the big truck, considering she was in her mid-seventies and barely five feet tall.

Waiting until there was no oncoming traffic, Ethel seized the wheel with one hand and began pushing Louise toward the open door with the other. They struggled against each other, neither gaining advantage, as the truck swerved back and forth between lanes, plowing a mailbox and sending a Corgi fleeing for cover.

The truck was bumping against the curb on the wrong side of the road as Ethel began pushing against Louise with both hands. Abruptly, Louise jerked the wheel slightly to the right as she pushed against her friend's ass with the other hand. Ethel went rolling out of the truck, hitting a passing tree. The resulting sound was not unlike someone jumping with both feet on a sheet of bubble wrap.

Louise slowed the truck to a stop back on the right side of the road, took a deep breath, and closed her eyes. She stayed that way for several minutes.

Moving to the back of the truck, Louise sat on a box and looked at Sue. When her friend had fallen over, the handle of the hammer, still buried firmly in her cranium, pushed against the driver's cheek, making it look like he was smiling wryly. Louise cocked her head and mimicked the look. He looked happy. Perhaps the perfect way to die was between a woman's legs, even if she was a septuagenarian.

As Louise sat on the box, she noticed a glint of something shiny in Sue's hand. She snatched it, and soon found herself giving the necklace quickie erections over and over. Smiling, she stowed it in her gown pocket, knowing it would be the perfect gift to get her a night of ecstasy.

Perching on the edge of the driver's seat again, Louise whipped the truck around to U-turn back toward the nursing home, almost T-boning a van on the way. Steadying the truck, she worked her way down the road, resisting the urge to go as fast as possible. A traffic stop, once the officer saw what had happened in the back of the truck, would end her chance at a good time.

As she pulled into the parking lot of the nursing home, Louise was surprised to not see emergency vehicles or nursing staff milling about outside. In general, they took great care of the residents, but they hadn't even noticed the three of them were gone. She parked the truck on the far side of the parking lot and made her way toward the front door.

Just as she got to the front door, Louise examined her hands and gown, amazed she had emerged spotless from the carnage. She cautiously entered the code and opened the front door, expecting hell from the nurses when they saw her come in unattended, but the nursing station was vacant. The Sex Gods were certainly on her side today.

Louise worked her way down the hallway toward Frankie's room, her finger flicking the necklace's penis up and down in her pocket. She arrived at Frankie's room and stepped inside, just in time to see a nurse pull a sheet over his head.

"Well, shit," Louise muttered. "That figures."

Author Notes

This story was written for a submission call for an anthology of stories where people make stupid decisions and pay the price for it. The Joe Lansdale characters Hap and Leonard were certainly inspiration for the submission call. My story was actually accepted, but the anthology never materialized. So I just recalled it and held it until I found the right home for it.

The inspiration for this story came from many of places, some of which I can't elaborate on, because those people might read this story. ☺ But somewhere along the way, I overheard a discussion about how often residents of nursing homes are caught having sex, and the answer was "more than you'd think."

From there I thought, to what extent would said residents go in order to get their world rocked? Would they do almost anything? Would they even kill?

Damn straight they would.

I tend to drop tidbits of humor and absurdities into many of my stories, but this is probably the one that has the most of both. I believe there's such a fine line between humor and horror, and the former is often used as a tension relief in the latter.

As a side note, the necklace I mentioned in this story is based in reality. There's an adult store near the University of Arkansas, and the owner is quite aware that many people who enter are nervous or embarassed to ask for help with the various products. So to help them relax, she will show her customers the necklace where, if she pulls on the chain at the bottom, the penis rises and falls. Definitely a local IYKYK thing.

Tweets I

We all gather at the park, picnic baskets and sweet tea in tow. Blankets spread out and covered with sandwiches, tater salad, and even Momma's famous cherry pie. She swaps recipes with Mrs. Todd from next door as I cock my head and watch that colored boy #dangle from the tree. #vss365

☠☠☠

He held his infant daughter close to his chest and tenderly kissed her forehead. The kisses continued, soft and gentle, as the fingers #tightly wrapped around his thumb relaxed and grew cold. #vss365

☠☠☠

At ten years old, Haley was adjusting to her new #normal with Mommy. No more Daddy. No more long sleeves at school to hide the cuts & bruises. No more bloodied & broken Mommy. Someone might find Daddy one day, but they would never find his hands, never find his head. #vss365.

☠☠☠

Bill & Linda's son, Cory, created a #schism in their marriage they could not overcome. From a lump on the monitor to a lump in her belly to a lump in his throat to a lump in the ground. Grief & anger & guilt & blame, too much pain to heal the wounds of death. #vss365

☠☠☠

Edwin stalked toward me, a hungry look in his eyes. He wanted me, but I had no desire for him. His life to me was monochromatic: silver spoon, silver tongue, silver hair on a silver fox. But it took me putting a #silver bullet between his eyes to drop him for good. #vss365

☠☠☠

The #pride circles its prey. Spaced, cautious, gaps too small for escape. The circle closes. The victim darts about, seeking freedom, denied each time by its attackers. Suddenly, they assault with fists & feet & calls of "Retard", tears & pain the victim's sole response. #vss365

☠☠☠

My wife was a #machine. Mother, wife, daughter, worker. Day after day, a powerhouse. But I never saw it, never said it. Told her she was nothing, a waste, not to bother me with her needs. Years of tears have now rusted that loving heart, & it's no longer mine to neglect. #vss365

☠☠☠

Every person has certain #dates etched in their mind, their soul, their very fiber. Every anniversary is a flood of joy, pain, loss, & love. For Henry, it was June 30, the day he put his wife in the earth. Equally important was July 3, when he brought her home again. #vss365

☠☠☠

On the street, there is no sense of #ubuntu or compassion that Cindy can see. Each person a loner, caring not beyond their reach. Opening throats with glass or skulls with pipes for a dry spot in an alley. Afraid to close her eyes, she never thought nine would be so hard. #vss365

☠☠☠

Blue eyes
Black heart
All I want
Nothing I need

Still I bend
Still I crawl
To your will
To your flesh

You tie my tongue
I tie you up
One more lick
One more kiss

Gasoline
Match
#Farewell

#vss365

☠☠☠

I #envy Tom's skill with a cleaver. I've learned so much at the butcher shop, how to find the joint, how to quickly cut through it. Even his saw skills are impeccable, & I'm in awe. He's been so pleased with my progress, tomorrow he lets me cut while he holds the men still. #vss365

☠☠☠

Mary gazes over the cotillion in her honor, the latest #debu-tante to come of age. This week she first bled, her mother proud, her father long cold in the ground. The coven gathers, chants, her blood the power in the spell. Nearby, the dirt smothering his corpse stirs. #vss365

☠ ☠ ☠

The pull, the #hunger, the absolute feral call for flesh drove her. She needed to feel the tender flesh rip in her maw, revel in the gush of hot blood down her throat, savor the orgasmic snap of bone, & suck the heavenly marrow. Silently she padded toward the playground. #vss365

☠ ☠ ☠

Rick pulled his meal to him, clutching it, growling at others who tried to steal it. No other could have it, this tasty morsel. It was meant to be savored, loved, relished. He lowered his head & slurped the sweet #ambrosia of blood as the infant went limp in his arms. #vss365

☠ ☠ ☠

I must #relax. It's my first day on the job, & I'm nervous. No previous experience. On the job training. Co-worker who yells & curses at me. I'm drenched in sweat, my muscles burn, but still I keep digging. After all, resurrectionists pay by the body, not by the hour. #vss365

☠ ☠ ☠

I've always done all I could for my children, pinching pennies where I could, anything to #scratch by. Many a time, they ate when I did not. I prayed for help & direction daily. But I wonder if I could have done more, as I hold their cold, blue corpses in my arms. #vss365

☠ ☠ ☠

I'm a wanderer, traveler, #nomad. Souls are my vehicle, to be used, burned, discarded. But my journey is ending, for this man has no soul. Not black or evil but absent. I look back on the centuries & smile at the damage I have done as he levels the pistol to his temple. #vss365

☠ ☠ ☠

Max's life with Rachel was the perfect, married life all they'd dreamed it to be. But it all #unraveled when Chloe arrived, a product of her parents' love. More & more Max wanted to spend time with Chloe, & he dreamed of those times as he pressed the pillow into Rachel's face. #vss365

☠ ☠ ☠

Bare feet, grimy & bleeding, shuffle along snow-cloaked streets, trails of pink & gray in their wake. Six-year-old Gracie winces at the pain & stops to wipe a tear. An #orphan of her own making, she thrusts the pistol into her mouth & adds another tick mark to the tally. #vss365

☠ ☠ ☠

Blue eyes, blue hands, blue feet, blue face. The girl in the alley is still, stripped of clothes, dignity, life. Mary cries as she looks down, remembering babies she sold for her habit. #Even grief won't stay her hand as she takes the girl's shirt, for warmth is life. #vss365

☠ ☠ ☠

"Merlot, #Bordeaux," Ella repeated in a sing-song, pouring wine over her head, down budding breasts, between thighs, finding every cut & scrape & bruise there. She stared at her father on the floor, he who'd done this to her, but the red shrouding his face was not wine. #vss365

All I can offer My Love is my #present, my future, my forever. She offers me the same, her love, her body, her heart. I treasure them forever, peeking daily at the jars filled with remembrances of her. Heart, fingers, lips, & those stunning blue eyes, now cloudy in death. #vss365

Hidden bruises on her back, yellow, brown, and purple. Red half-moon frowns on her arm from vice-grip hands. One eye begins to #swell. Terror when he is home; broken wings fail to fly when he is not. Blade tucked along her forearm, she approaches Daddy's sleeping form. #vss365

He lay beside his wife, fingertips circling her #belly button, the timer popped out. They giggled and smooched when they felt the tiny kick, joy overcoming them. Tomorrow was arrival day, but she would return home with only sorrow, a flat stomach, and barren arms. #vss365

Back of a palm on her infant's forehead, scalded by his #fiery heat. Lips pressed to his, she draws the fire into herself, cooling and healing him. His eyes flutter and he smiles. Alas, just a dream. So she holds the inferno of his body to hers and waits for the end. #vss365

The man tugged the #brim of his cap & lowered his chin, hiding his eyes. He ogled the giggling young girls at the playground. One, about four years old, bounced off to chase a butterfly, her mother distracted. He slipped away after the girl, the last she would be seen. #vss365

☠ ☠ ☠

Pain numbed by morphine, Todd watched her flay the skin of his arms, chest, legs. Slowly stretched, relaxed, stretched again. Flesh #nailed to the wall, his gaze met that of a man pinned opposite him, eyes pleading for release, just one more butterfly in her collection. #vss365

☠ ☠ ☠

Teetering on the railing, ground six stories below, Kat locks fingers with the specter of her man, gazes into his eyes, & blows him a kiss. Leaning forward, scent of his cologne in her mind, asphalt rising to caress her, she and her love will finally #always be together. #vss365

☠ ☠ ☠

The child peered down the dark stairs with #dread, but still the whispers came. She crept down, inch by inch, until light had fled away. One match, two, three, & the wood stove woke to greet her. She crawled into its warm embrace & escaped the cold of her Daddy's touch. #vss365

☠ ☠ ☠

Thirty-penny nails. Long, sturdy, reliable, & they stayed where you put them. Mae had been #blind to their usefulness for too long. Now, clarity was hers. She smiled at her sleeping husband, then pressed the nail gun to his temple & fired. No more wandering eyes for him. #vss365

☠☠☠

Your #words are nothing, promises that fail, stagnate, wither on the vine of hope. I'm immune to your charms & stunning cornflower eyes your smile never reaches. Here, I'll save your eyes & voice in this box, open it daily, watch them rot, & revel in their putrid aroma. #vss365

☠☠☠

A nudge with a toe, a verbal #prompt, a light kick. No response. The young girl kneels beside the still form & twirls her finger inside the hole she made behind her mother's ear. Finally free from the icy fingers under her dress, the girl frowns. Now who will fix dinner? #vss365

Author Notes

As I noted in the preface, I love super-short fiction, because it's such a challenge to pack an entire story into an extremely limited space. When that length is measured in characters not words, it's even more extreme.

Most of these micro-stories are pretty straightforward, but I wanted to touch on the very first one, the one about the lynching. When I posted that on Twitter, I got several hateful comments and even more DMs with people saying I'm racist, etc.

But here's the thing. I'm always trying to tell the story of the underdog, those in the margins or minorities, and those just flat-out ignored.

Part of our nation's history, especially in the South, is racism and lynchings. And anyone who would say that lynchings weren't a social event many folks attended and, yes, even packed a picnic basket for, need to read up on history. Things have indeed gotten better in many ways, but that tweet was just a minute glimpse into that place in time.

Ultimately, any hate I received was more than balanced out by the messages I got from people of color, thanking me for being willing to tell that story, as brief as it was. It's not my lived experience, but it often is theirs. And any light that shines on it can't hurt.

"Love and Infamy"

Dragging a fork through the red and blue frosting on her slice of birthday cake, Edith Watson muttered to herself. "Seven minutes. Seven damn minutes."

Her eyes rose to look at her older twin sister, Alice, who was receiving congratulatory hugs and kisses from nurses and doctors at the nursing home, all celebrating Alice's status as the oldest living person. Edith shook her head slowly. "Seven damn minutes".

One of the nurses briefly noticed Edith's morose demeanor and beamed at her, then returned her attention to the local celebrity. Edith returned a wan smile and flicked frosting across the table, some landing on the middle one of the "115" in the center of the birthday cake.

Edith and her sister were named after the wives of Theodore Roosevelt, who was president when they were born. Naturally, Alice was named after the first wife and Edith after the second. The younger sister had long ago become accustomed to finishing second to her sibling.

A sudden motion pulled Edith from her reverie, as she realized her wheelchair was being moved. While neither she nor her sister required a wheelchair, the nursing home insisted, likely a combination of concerns over liability and maintaining celebrity status. It wasn't lost on Edith that the wheelchairs weren't needed until the 117-year-old lady in Italy kicked the bucket last year, putting 114-year-old Alice in the limelight.

Edith was wheeled next to Alice, who was busy mugging for a television reporter. After some cajoling, Edith reluctantly kissed her sister on the cheek, holding it long enough for a round of flashes from staff cell phones. Following the kiss, Edith wiped her mouth on her sleeve, hoping nobody noticed.

The celebration lasted a couple hours, until the staff finally noticed the sisters were fading fast, victims of exhaustion. Slowly the other residents were wheeled back to their rooms until only Alice and Edith remained. They looked at each other, and Alice smiled. Placing her hand on her sister's, she whispered, "I love you, sis. Always have."

Edith held her sister's gaze, a tear slowly creeping down her cheek. "I know, girl. I know."

"I never asked for this fame, you know that, right? I wish people would include you more, but they don't seem to be interested." Alice sighed. "I'm sorry. Really I am. You deserve time in the spotlight too."

Nodding slowly, Edith pondered her sister's words. Was there any honesty behind them? Or was she just trying to play big sister and help her baby sister feel better? Shrugging slowly, Edith answered. "I know, Alice. I know."

Soon they were being wheeled to their room, where Alice enjoyed the bed with the better view. She could see the pond and park benches behind the nursing home, while Edith's view was obstructed by a fenced-in air conditioning unit. The nurses took good care of the sisters as always, doling out their evening medications and tucking them into bed, railings on each side raised to prevent accidental falls.

Edith lay quietly in her bed thinking about the evening, her thoughts turning frequently to her sister. Perhaps she had been unfair all these years. Alice never made Edith feel like a second-class citizen. Most often that was an albatross Edith placed around her own neck. Her thoughts waffled back and forth, tears accompanying each change in heart.

Eventually Edith was serenaded by her sister's light snoring, and she smiled to herself. There was comfort in that sound, knowing they'd both successfully survived another day. She sat up and inched her way to the foot of her bed until she was past the end of the railing, then slowly slid off the bed until she was standing.

Carefully making her way to the other side of the divided room, Edith stood beside her sleeping sister, cocked her head, and smiled.

She scooted a footstool beside the bed and climbed onto it, nearly falling backward in the process.

Finally perched on top of the short stool, Edith leaned forward and kissed her sleeping sister on the forehead. "I love you, Alice," she whispered, then placed the pillow she'd carried over Alice's face and fell on top of it.

Alice's hands flew up in panic, clutching at anything she could secure, her weak hands attempting to secure purchase before finally clenching the sleeve of Edith's gown. The death throes quickened then slowly subsided until Alice's grip loosened but never let go.

Edith lovingly removed her sister's hand from her gown and laid it gently on the bed. She slid off the top of the pillow, missing the stool but managing to land roughly on the floor. After moving the stool back under her sister's bed, Edith made her way back to her own.

Finally settled down and under the covers, Edith found herself too excited to sleep. She smiled to herself, imagining all the cameras, interviews, hugs, kisses, and attention she would receive as she reveled in her fifteen minutes of fame. Near dawn, she finally relaxed enough to doze off, a smile firmly in place as she slipped into a slumber from which she would never awaken.

Author Notes

The inspiration for this story was a news article about the oldest person in the world at the time, who I believe lived in Japan, dying. It talked about the notoriety they had and how that would pass to the new World's Oldest Living Person.

That got me thinking, what if there were someone who really wanted that fame and notoriety? What if they were so close to having it, but they were held back by someone they knew? And what if it were their older twin? How much closer could you get to them?

Of course, the next step was, what would they be willing to do to gain that notoriety? And the story just developed from there.

"Coffee and Pie with a Friend"

A single shot through the temple. That much is true."

Dieter held his right forefinger to his own temple for a moment as if to underscore the statement, then returned his attention to the steaming cup of coffee in front of him. His thumb began slowly tapping against the side of the cup, creating small ripples inside.

I marveled silently at how I had come to be sitting here in the kitchen of Dieter Günther, bodyguard and trusted confidant of Adolf Hitler and the sole remaining survivor from Hitler's inner circle. I had learned through a German magazine Dieter lived outside Cleveland, and I knew I had to make the nine hour drive from St. Louis to meet him. There we sat, in his kitchen, sipping coffee his caregiver had poured.

I considered his last comment for a moment. "So, if it's that simple, why did you agree to meet? What else is there to tell?" I leaned forward, resting my chin on folded hands, waiting for him to continue.

His gaze lifted from his coffee cup, and he held it on a point over my shoulder for a while. I turned to identify the object of his gaze, but met only our reflection in the kitchen window.

"*Ja*, there is more to the story." Dieter inhaled deeply, letting it out slowly through his nose. "My days remaining on earth are now measured in weeks, not years. Perhaps it is time to tell this story.

"*Mein Führer* was a powerful man. Very powerful. People of all walks are drawn to such power, like moths to a flame. Some people fall victim to such power. Others feed from it, in different ways.

"And his charisma. Never have I known someone like that. Power. Charisma. Alas, absolute power corrupts absolutely, as they say. And *Mein Führer* was no exception."

Coffee splashed from Dieter's cup as the rhythmic tapping of his thumb against the side became more forceful. Hot liquid struck his hand, which he quickly jerked away.

"Detractors of *Mein Führer* are fond of saying he was unable to please a woman, unable to perform as a man. They say he was—" Dieter paused, his scalded hand moving in a circle as he searched for the right word.

"Impotent?" I offered.

"*Ja*. Impotent. Must be a French word. Never understood the language." His thumb began caressing the cup now, slowly, as if imagining a past love. "But it is not true. *Nein*, he was a lover of the ladies, and they of him. Who would not want to be close to such a powerful man? To say they had known him intimately, in bed, where men are most vulnerable?

"He was not abnormal in his sexual desires, from what I heard. Merely prolific. *Ja*, definitely prolific."

"But what about Eva Braun?"

Dieter considered this and smiled for the first time during our meeting. "Eva was but a child, almost twenty-five years younger. She was as infatuated with him as the other ladies were. There was something about her *Mein Führer* was attracted to, but I know not what it was.

"But he would not touch her as a man would touch a woman, perhaps afraid he would spoil her innocence, her purity. Eva was there because it was expected of him to produce an heir. Who would not love Eva as the mother of the Reich's heir? But if it had happened, it would have been with another woman, the child raised as Eva's."

Slowly rocking his neck from side to side to pop it, Dieter paused briefly then continued. "It was experienced women *Mein Führer* desired the most. He did not have patience to teach and explain. He merely wanted to enjoy. Discretion was not his strength in that regard. Yet a scandal was never a worry. Who would tell of having lain with him, knowing it would destroy the image of him and Eva? They would surely have been put to death.

"Many believe *Mein Führer* had syphilis, that this was the cause of his decline in health. Had they known of his appetite in bed, it would have only served to strengthen that belief." Dieter exhaled slowly through pursed lips. "But that was not it. *Nein*, not at all."

His gaze fixed beyond my shoulder again, but this time I waited patiently for him to continue. His caregiver arrived, asking if we wanted something to eat, perhaps some pecan pie. I accepted her hospitality, as did Dieter.

"As *Mein Führer's* most trusted bodyguard," he continued, "I saw almost all parts of his life. Much of it went to that shallow fiery grave with him, as it should. Perhaps this should too." As he stared at his front door, I wondered if Dieter wished he were in another place or time. Soon he returned his attention to his coffee cup, as if it were his audience.

"Nineteen forty-one. That was the beginning of the end for *Mein Führer*. Since he often had women in his bed chambers, he would confide in me so he would not be interrupted. I was the one who usually delivered messages to him, and I was his bodyguard, so it was natural he told me.

"He had not been sleeping well for a month or so, so I did not wish to wake him. I worried for his health, and talk among the staff had already begun. *Mein Führer* was no longer a young man, so a decline was inevitable, but none of us wished to consider his mortality.

"One April night, I entered his chambers to update him on the invasion of Greece. *Unternehmen Marita*, as it was called, was a tremendous success. We were just days from taking Athens, and I knew *Mein Führer* wished to hear the glorious news.

"Just as I opened the door, I noticed a woman astride *Mein Führer*. In the darkness, it appeared she was almost floating, as if wings were holding her up. But I dismissed this as fatigue on my part and quickly closed the door, apologizing profusely. I was certain this interruption would result in a bullet through my skull."

The caregiver returned with our pie. "*Danke,* Heidrun," he said while smiling. "Heidrun is a wonderful help to me. I've known her for many, many years. I am blessed to have her assistance."

Sliding a forkful of pie into his mouth and chewing slowly, Dieter nodded his appreciation. "Very good. Very good indeed. It is America's number one contribution to cuisine, and Heidrun has done a wonderful job learning to make it. But heaven is her strudel. Perhaps on your next visit." He smiled and nodded at me, and we each finished our respective slice of pie in silence.

"I waited for a moment, conflicted between interrupting *Mein Führer* and knowing he would wish to hear the good news about Greece." Dieter wiped the corner of his mouth with a napkin, then folded it and returned it to the table. "I knocked softly, but no reply came. Again I knocked softly. When no answer came, I opened the door to find only *Mein Führer* in the room, sound asleep. The woman was not there.

"I gently woke him to tell him the glorious news of Greece, and it was clear he was in a deep sleep prior to my arrival. He expressed gratitude for the news and went back to sleep."

Dieter pinched the bridge of his nose and closed his eyes. Taking another deep breath, he went on. "The next morning, *Mein Führer* told me of this most wonderful dream he had, of this beautiful sexual creature who had sated him completely. In many ways, he was much like other men, wishing to brag of conquests, even imaginary ones. He then left my company in search of a maid who was a regular in his bed, hoping to release some excess energy.

"I did not see it at the time, because it was so gradual, but under the perspective of time, it is clear as a bright Bavarian day. Over the next four years, *Mein Führer's* sexual appetite slowly declined. It would be easy to say it was simply his age, as he was in his fifties by then. That may have been partially true. But it began at that time. I know that now.

"*Mein Führer* would also on occasion tell me of that same dream, which would come to him now and again. It was always the same beautiful creature who visited him, and each time he would be more and more tired in the morning. The evidence of the power of this dream was in his laundry, as I heard the maids tell it."

He stopped to pop his neck again, a little more audibly than before. When his silence persisted as I made notes, I looked up and noticed Dieter looking beyond my shoulder, into the darkness again. This time I could not resist looking, but again, I saw only our reflection. Opening my mouth to inquire, I decided not to, afraid it would break the spell of his tale.

Taking advantage of the pause in Dieter's story, I studied him as he gazed into his coffee cup, perhaps searching for courage to continue. Like anyone of his advanced age, his skin was thin like parchment, wisps of white hair framing his crown. His nose was more pronounced in his golden years than in the pictures I had seen of him wearing his *Führerbegleitkommando* uniform.

I also noted the telltale pucker of a bullet wound in his left forearm and wondered what other scars he sported, be they physical or mental, healed or raw. My respect for this man and his survival into his nineties increased sharply.

Finally, after taking a few sips of his recently refilled coffee, Dieter continued with his story. "Look up the history using your Google. Find out when the beginning of the end was for our Reich. *Mein Führer's* decline began shortly after I stumbled into that nighttime encounter. His mind began to go. A few months after what I witnessed, he deliberately went against his generals' advice and invaded Russia. The Reich army was divided and never the same again."

Closing his eyes and inhaling in deeply, Dieter plunged on. "It was the third night of our stay in the *Führerbunker*. January of nineteen forty-five. Late in the evening, I approached *Mein Führer's* bedroom, careful not to wake Eva, who had fallen asleep in the study while reading a novel. I opened his door without knocking, as he had told me he would only be resting, not sleeping.

"As I opened the door, I again saw this creature mounted on our leader. She was at once beautiful and terrifying. Her hands were folded over her head as she moved, and I was able to see all of her beauty. Her curves were perfect, the hint of a breast visible.

"Yet, what held my sight was not her beauty, but her long black wings, much like those of a giant bat, stretched beyond the width of the bed. With each rocking motion, her wings closed partially then extended to their full length, popping softly like leather."

A visible shiver went through him as he paused, eyes closed. "Then she turned and met my gaze, making no effort to run away as before. Her eyes were completely black, no white at all, except for a tiny point of red in the center. She stared at me and smiled as she continued to move, and I could stand there no longer.

"I closed the door too loudly, waking Eva. I apologized and, not wanting her to see what I had, told her the Goebbels children had been asking about her. She left to check on them. I left the study hoping the children were indeed still awake."

Dieter paused for a moment, nodding at Heidrun and lifting his coffee cup to get it topped off. I wondered at her lack of surprise hearing his story. Perhaps it was no surprise to her.

Holding his now-full cup close to his mouth, he blew across the top to cool the coffee but put it down without drinking. I expected him to again stare over my shoulder, but his focus remained on his cup.

"*Mein Führer* told me of his dream the next morning, as usual. But there was sadness in his story, almost fatigue, as if the visitor was no longer welcome. That was the last time he told me of such a dream. It was as if she had drained all the power she desired from *Mein Führer*, and she had nothing left to gain.

"The remaining months of his life were filled with a depression as he moved from one task, one meeting, one day to another. Those around him rightfully believed he was worried of the future of the Reich and of his people, but I knew there was more. I knew he both longed for and dreaded any future visits from that creature."

Dieter sipped from his coffee, wincing as the heat stung his lips and mouth, but he continued to drink until almost half the cup had been drained. He picked at a few crumbs on his plate, but made no effort to eat them. Instead he just sat there for several minutes, his thumb bouncing against the table top. I had just started to gather my notebook and pen, certain the story was over, when Dieter began talking again.

"I do not know if that terrible creature returned, but I suspect she did not. I refused to enter *Mein Führer's* bed chambers again, instead asking others to relay messages, pretending to be too busy. Fortunately, he rarely slept those last few months, so he was most often in his study or the conference room.

"His fifty-sixth birthday was celebrated, but nobody really felt it. We all knew the end was near. When he killed his beloved Shepherd, Blondi, to test the cyanide, I knew he had lost any hope for the future. Just ten days after his birthday, *Mein Führer* ended his own life."

His thumb finally still, Dieter sat quietly for several minutes, biting down gently on his lower lip, as if remembering something painful or, more likely, hoping to not remember. Draining his coffee cup, he finally looked up and held my gaze.

"Did you know the night *Mein Führer* died was *Walpurgisnacht*? Witches are said to hold great bonfires on that night. Is it mere chance a pyre was made of our beloved *Führer* and Eva that very night?" Dieter simply looked at me, as if letting me form my own opinion.

"I wish Eva did not have to die. She had no part in any of the Reich's plans, only——. What is the expression? Guilt by association?" Seeing me nod, he continued. "Eva was a truly innocent *fräulein*. Her only fault was catching the fancy of the most powerful man in the Reich.

"But *Mein Führer* was right that she could not belong to anyone else. Who would want her? She would be an outcast the remainder of her life. But she gladly gave her life for her Reich and her husband."

Dieter's eyes briefly flicked from mine to over my shoulder and back. "And now, my friend, I must retire for the evening. I have not the energy I did as a young man of the Reich. God has blessed me with good health in my old age, but I still tire easily. And I cannot pretend I have slept well in the days leading up to our meeting. This was not an easy decision." Again, his eyes briefly glanced over my shoulder.

"Remember, my friend, history is written by the victors. Or in my case, the survivors. None will believe this tale, and yet, it was one I needed to tell. It will make a wonderful campfire story for your grandchildren, should you be blessed enough to have any. Sadly, I have not had the pleasure, as the story I have told you has kept me from laying with a woman at all."

We both stood and shook hands, offering each other pleasantries and promises to see one another again. I also thanked Heidrun for her hospitality, but she only smiled weakly in response.

Suddenly Dieter's heels clicked together sharply, and I half expected a *sieg heil* salute, but he only offered a shallow bow. "Be well, my friend," he whispered and opened the door for me, moving well for a man of his age.

As I opened my car door, I turned to wave goodbye to Dieter, but he had already shut out the outside world. On the ride back to my hotel, I couldn't help but believe tonight Dieter would have a wonderful yet terrifying dream. And it would be his last.

Author Notes

This story was submitted for an anthology of Nazi-related un-dead/supernatural stories. The editor actually liked the story, but he said he didn't think it would be clear to readers that the antagonist was a succubus. One of those times where picking something that wasn't a zombie, vampire, or werewolf hurt me.

I've long been fascinated by Hitler. Not with admiration, since he was unquestionably a horrible person, but by all the points in his life where if something minor had gone another way, how different the world would be today. With that in mind, I've read many accounts of Nazi Germany, not just regarding Hitler, but the people who surrounded him.

In this story, Dieter is an amalgamation of many people I've read about: Hitler's valet, bodyguard, secretary, etc. Obviously, this story had to be told by someone in his inner circle.

Heidrun was named after a real person, namely Heidrun Goeb-bels, the youngest daughter of Joseph Goebbels, Hitler's chief pro-pogandist. Unfortunately, the real-life Heidrun suffered the same fate as all the Goebbels children, drugged by morphine then given cyanide capsules.

I enjoy putting in real-world anchors to a fictitious story, and this has several, including the invasion of Greece in early 1945. As a reader, that adds believability to a story, so I try to include those tidbits when I can.

"Decisions, Decisions"

We knew they were out there. The persistent scratching at the bedroom door, shadows visible under it, and that putrid stench emanating everywhere. But we didn't dare put a blanket across the bottom of the door to staunch the odor. The motion from the shadows was how we knew where they were.

For the last couple years, I had nagged David to install a trellis below our second-story bedroom window so I could grow some ivy. Now I was glad he hadn't yet, as it kept the monsters from reaching us from that window. But it also prevented us from escaping through the window.

David leaned his weight against the door, hoping it would be enough if the creatures tried to break through. They were quicker than we first thought, and we wouldn't make that mistake again. As he leaned, David inspected a long scratch on his forearm and hand, a fetid mixture of blood and pus already dripping from his fingers. On his other shoulder he balanced a 12-gauge.

He wiggled the fingers of his infected hand, but they seemed to have a mind of their own. "It's already happening, Grace."

I didn't know what to say, so I just nodded.

We had no idea how these monsters were made. Zombies, some viral outbreak, aliens, it didn't matter. All we knew was they wanted us dead.

They had a taste for stomachs and livers of all things. I glanced out the window and watched several feed on Mrs. Thompkins in her front yard next door. Their gray and purple faces were bathed in her blood, and one held a piece of her entrails before taking a vigorous bite. The creature paused long enough to notice me watching, and I had to look away. I hated those rheumy eyes with white pupils. At least the monsters making a buffet of Mrs. Thompkins were far enough away we couldn't smell their rotting flesh.

A loud thud echoed through the room as one, or maybe more, of the creatures launched into the door. David bounced forward a bit, but quickly reinforced his brace, scooting his feet away to lower his center of gravity. The doorknob even wiggled, as if they were hoping we had forgotten to lock it. Whatever was creating these creatures didn't hurt their intelligence at all. In fact, they appeared to become pack animals, hunting with greater efficiency, even if it meant sharing their meals.

David grimaced and put more weight against the door. I could see he was canting to the right, and I feared he was getting weaker.

He was my hero, the man I had always hoped for. His protective instincts were impeccable, always sensing what needed to be done to make life better for us, whether it meant a security system, the shotgun he held, or even working a second job to give us breathing room with the mortgage.

"How are you doing, David?" I chewed my lip after asking, afraid of the answer.

"Not good, Grace." He moved his fingers again, and it was obvious his control was decreasing. "Not good at all." He held my gaze. "We gotta find a way out, Love. We have to."

I nodded, my default behavior when at a loss for words.

Fingers slipped under the door then slid back and forth, looking for something, anything to grasp. Soon, a second set of fingers appeared, also searching for a target. When they found nothing both hands disappeared.

David smiled and scooted his feet closer to the door.

"Don't. It's too risky," I implored, worried the creatures would be able to reach him.

A moment later, fingers appeared under the door again, and just when they wriggled and reached for David's pant leg, he lifted a boot and stomped hard on the fingers. The resulting crunch was somehow both satisfying and sickening. He leaned his weight onto that foot, and the door bounced wildly as the creature tried to free itself. Finally, David lifted his foot, and the fingers disappeared. He moved his feet away from the door and leaned again, but this time a little lower than before.

"How could you, David?" My eyes were wide in shock.

"What? They were just begging to be broken. They asked for it."

"I just don't see how you can be that violent." I looked away and crossed my arms.

"Wow, really? You know all bets are off, right? All that matters is us getting out of here alive." David shifted his weight. "I'll do what I have to do to protect you. I always do."

"Yeah, but—" I looked at him long and hard, but he refused to look away, his face absent of emotion. "Never mind."

Some unknown amount of time passed in silence as I paced around the room, not knowing what to say or do. David, for his part, kept his weight against the door but was inching his way down the surface as he weakened. His hair was now sopping wet, and his khaki shirt dark with sweat stains.

Soon, he could no longer support his weight, and he collapsed to the floor, seated but still leaning against the door. As expected, fingers shot out under the door, reaching for his belt, but finding no purchase, they withdrew.

"I'm losing it, Love. I—" Turning his head, he vomited a foul mixture of green and red. Blood, phlegm, and whatever food had been left in his stomach added to the overpowering reek in the room. He looked at the mess, then at me, closing his eyes. "It won't be long, Grace," he said, eyes still closed.

Setting the shotgun on the floor, he scooted it toward me. His eyes opened as much as they could, and he focused on me, but not without significant effort. "You need to save yourself. Soon I will be as dangerous to you as they are. And I'm already in the same room."

As part of his never-ending mission to protect me, David had taught me to shoot many firearms, from the shotgun to a 1911, P226, and even an AR-15. But this was different. The only targets I had ever shot were paper ones at the range or beer bottles and soup cans in the pasture behind our house. I had never even been hunting, much less killed anything.

David had just asked me to murder him, the man I loved, the man I promised I would grow old and die with. I couldn't do it. I just shook my head and backed away, speechless.

"Come on, Grace, you know it's the best way."

I was unable to meet his eyes at this point. There was no way I could bring myself to pick up the gun, much less pull the trigger.

Then a voice floated from the other side of the door, one we dreaded but knew would come eventually. "Mommy? Daddy? We love you."

My eyes filled with tears, and I sat hard on the bed, sobs racking my body. As long as I could, I had pushed out of my head who the monsters were, but no longer. No matter what they were now, I still viewed them as my babies, the ones I had given birth to, raised, clothed, fed, and above all, protected.

And now they wanted me dead. Wanted *us* dead.

"Mommy? Mommy, hold us."

David looked up at me and nodded slowly. Reaching for the shotgun, he used it as a crutch to lift himself to his feet. He swayed, but managed to keep his balance.

It dawned on me what he had in mind. "David, you can't. You just can't." My body shook again as I blubbered.

As if on cue, a soft voice drifted from the hallway. "Daddy, we love you. Play on the swings with us, Daddy."

"It's the only way, Grace. You know in your heart it is. They are no longer our children. Ellie, Tommy, and Katie are gone."

I nodded again. I hated it. Hated him. But I knew he was right.

David wobbled until he was near the door then leaned his head against it as if gathering strength. Reaching into his pocked, he removed two more shells and placed them between his teeth.

Without a word or backward glance, he moved beside the door, unlocked it, and opened it just enough to squeeze through. Ellie met my eyes for a split second before the door slammed shut behind David.

I heard Tommy start to say, "Daddy", but his voice was cut short by the thunderous report of the shotgun. My other two children shrieked, but one was interrupted by another blast. A spent shell rolled under the door.

The sound of David reloading his shotgun was interrupted by his intense scream, and I froze, a mixture of fear and dread overcoming me. I heard a sound like a dropped watermelon, which was followed by the sound of the shotgun firing again. Then silence.

I crept toward the door, drawn by the faint sound of breathing. "David?" I probed.

"Don't, Grace."

I stopped in the middle of the room, unsure what to do. Standing there, I listened to his ragged breathing, listened as it got more and more shallow.

"I love you, Grace."

One final shotgun blast. The light under the door was extinguished by my hero's crumpled form, and his blood flowed as if he were reaching for me one last time.

Author Notes

This story was another that emerged from a what-if scenario, mainly what would happen if the zombies you were hiding from were your children? How hard would any decision to dispatch them be?

Though this was written in the height of *The Walking Dead* popularity, I had never seen an episode of it since zombies were never my jam. I didn't watch *TWD* until years later. Of course, the monsters in this story were never clearly labeled, whether as zombies or otherwise.

At the core of this story is the parental knowledge that most of us would gladly sacrifice ourselves to save our children. Of course, it also includes the willingness to save your spouse or life partner.

Drabbles

They called Betty antisocial. Distant eyes and pursed lips when other children were around, fists clenching and relaxing over and over and over.

"We need to get her a therapist," mom told her hubby. "She shouldn't be like this at six. People will start talking, and we don't need that right now. People will think we're poor parents and won't invite us to parties."

Betty heard her words, understood their misplaced and selfish concerns.

But she had a remedy. Here a nap ended with an ice pick, there a hair dryer dropped into the hot tub.

Easy peasy lemon squeezy.

☠ ☠ ☠

Robbie's eyes bore into the back of his Dad's head. For three years now, he's seen that hair, that face, those hands, and the rest of his body.

At seven, Robbie came to live with his new dad. Walking home from the park, Dad gave him a ride to his new home. Since that time, they shared a home, meals, TV, even a bed.

Now, as Dad sleeps, Robbie shuffles behind him and stares at the side of his neck, the curve toward his shoulder, the indention behind his collarbone, then Robbie buries the blade behind the bone and twists.

Author Notes

Neither of these were part of any particular calls. As I've said elsewhere, I love micro-fiction because of the necessary word economy. Both of these were just ideas that popped up, and I wondered if I could do each of them in exactly 100 words.

"Leaving Kléber Station"

As the last metro from Kléber zoomed out of sight, Bellocq flipped his hand in mock frustration while keeping the dazed woman balanced against his side. He pulled her tighter, leaned against the white tile wall, and watched the subway train disappear.

"*Fils de pute*," he muttered, furthering the ruse in case anyone was near enough to hear.

The woman, a college-aged brunette named Megan, reached weakly with one hand to move a lock of hair from her face, missing it entirely. Her hand fell to her side, and Bellocq kissed her gently on the forehead.

"It's good, sweetheart. We will be home soon." Another tender kiss to her forehead.

Bellocq had met Megan at a brasserie near Boissière metro station. He presumed she was a foreigner trying to have a stereotypical fling with a Frenchman, based on her checking out the ass of every man walking past, combined with her butchered greeting, which sounded more like "Bun-jore". Just the same, he decided if she wanted an adventure while in Paris, he could fulfill that wish.

So he had slid onto the bar stool beside her and struck up a conversation. His unkempt dark black hair and brown eyes seemed to hold women when he talked to them. A perpetual five o'clock shadow added to the bad boy image.

While fluent in English, Bellocq pretended to search for the right words to converse in her language, all of which he hoped added to his charm. Based on her reaction, it did.

Megan let him buy her a drink, then she returned the favor, and soon both had downed several glasses of Cabernet Sauvignon.

Enough, in fact, that Megan apparently never noticed when Bellocq quit refilling his glass while making sure hers stayed topped off. She offered no resistance when he suggested they leave so he could show her what a Frenchman was truly capable of in the sheets, although he had to carry her down the stairs into the metro station. They took the train to Kléber, where they now stood.

The soft melody of an alto saxophone drifted through the hallways, but its beauty was counter-punched by the acrid odor of urine. Bellocq had no patience for men who couldn't hold their liquor, as he believed it to be a sign of weakness. As he scowled at the thought of being that out of control, the music cut off, as if the busker too had realized it was time to go home. Bellocq was left with only the woman at his side and the smell of piss.

As the station grew quiet, Bellocq worked to maintain his patience, knowing he had to be sure the metro was empty. Convinced this was the case, he reached into his pocket with the hand not supporting Megan and clicked a button on the device there. It would activate a transmitter under the platform lip, and a signal would disrupt the security cameras to nothing but static, in case anyone were to look at the video later.

Bellocq weaved to the edge of the platform with Megan then laid her down gently, her bag of souvenirs serving as a pillow. Hopping to the ground beside the rail, he rolled Megan onto his shoulders in a fireman's carry. He eyed the bag of souvenirs, contemplating abandoning them, then decided there might be something of value he could use or sell and grabbed it with his free hand.

As the near-darkness swallowed him, Bellocq shifted the bag to the hand holding Megan's legs and clicked the device's button again with his now-free hand. He hoped the security cameras were re-enabled, but he had to trust the process.

Besides, he had other priorities. Feeling Megan's soft breasts against his back aroused him, and he couldn't wait to show her what he was capable of.

From the end of the exit tunnel marked "*Sortie*", Chloe Carron watched the two figures disappear into the darkness. She had been working on the cleaning crew for the last six months, and several times she had seen the monitors in the security office turn to static for several minutes before returning to their normal view. It would have been easy to dismiss as a technical malfunction, but it only took a couple times for her to realize it always happened within minutes of the last train leaving for Étoile.

When she saw the static tonight, she hurried as quietly as possible toward the platform. Not long after it had grown still, Chloe heard movement far down the platform. She peeked around the corner of the tunnel and spotted the man lowering the woman to the platform, jumping to the ground, and carrying her away.

Chloe looked at her phone. It was almost one-thirty a.m., and she had to finish her sweeping and emptying the trash by two, or her boss would be on her ass. She would have to check it out the next time, if the static returned. Glancing toward the dark subway tunnel again, she hoped the girl would be fine. There were a lot of sick bastards in this city, and Chloe hoped the woman hadn't found one.

☠ ☠ ☠

Bellocq walked toward Étoile as far as he could by the light from Kléber station. The tunnels had intermittent lights, but not enough to see where he was walking. He used his free hand to find his way by sliding it across the wall and using the flashlight app on his phone as needed to help him pick his way through the tunnel.

It would take a while to walk to his crew's hideout, and he sang the latest song from his favorite rapper, Lomepal. His singing sucked, and he knew it, but the only one who could complain out here was Megan, and she didn't have a damned thing to say right now.

He got through several songs before a sharp "*Arrête!*" interrupted him. Bellocq stopped immediately, not wanting to give his lookouts a reason to be suspicious.

"It's just me."

"I knew that, Bellocq. We can pick out your shitty singing anywhere." A cigarette lighter sprang to life, illuminating the face of a young man of nineteen, sporting a scruffy, dirty-blonde hairdo and a face full of stubble. He wore a blue bandana around his neck, which he liked to pull over his face to mimic the bandits he saw on American television.

"Louis? Where's Dylan? He's supposed to be watching this end." Bellocq shifted the package on his shoulder and rocked his neck back and forth, popping it.

Louis gestured vaguely behind him. "He had to go shit. Knowing him, he's sneaking a cigarette too, since we can't have them while we're watching."

Bellocq nodded, shifted his parcel again, and continued toward their hideout. It only took them another three minutes to reach it.

Between the stations were several rows of abandoned subway cars, and Bellocq's crew had made a home behind the last one. They all had alarms on their phones to notify them when the first trains would start running each day, and they valued the four or so hours they had the tunnel to themselves. Occasionally a vandal or graffiti artist would wander into their domain, but they never left. At least, not alive.

As he slipped behind the last car, Bellocq stopped to admire the reason they had picked this location. Where the floor met the wall, a ten-foot section of mushrooms had grown, glowing a soft, fluorescent blue, each pulsing every few seconds. Bellocq resisted the call to nibble on one and laid Megan on a pallet of flattened cardboard boxes.

Several years ago, Paul Macron had stumbled across the fungi as he was wandering the tunnels. Though he didn't know why, he couldn't resist the urge to sample one. He quickly learned of their power as his eyes adapted to the darkness, his muscles rippled and tensed, and he sprouted the hardest erection he'd ever had.

Macron moved his crew's base of operations to this location, and they all enjoyed the mushrooms, which grew back in a matter of hours. They also learned of the downside to this new wonder drug, in that they would be impotent for almost a week after indulging. A guy could grab the most talented whore from Place Pigalle, and she could work her magic, but nothing would happen. It would be like she was playing with a dead worm. So they paced themselves, only indulging when they had someone ready to play with.

During one such playtime, Bellocq had wandered to their base and found Macron, eyes closed, with Bellocq's girlfriend bent over a makeshift bench, taking full advantage of the mushrooms' gift. Unfortunately for Macron, the increased strength and power didn't prevent Bellocq from slicing his throat open with the sharp edge of a folded Coke can. When the woman looked over her shoulder, thinking the hot liquid on her ass was from Macron shooting his load, Bellocq buried the impromptu blade in her right eye, then her left.

Bellocq took control of the crew then, and it only took one look at the dead couplers for them to realize Bellocq was capable of things they were not. Most were petty criminals, adept at lifting wallets and phones from unsuspecting tourists on the subway or running rigged shell games near Sacré-Cœur. None of them had so much as broken someone's finger, much less killed two people in seconds with an aluminum can.

None of them knew where the mushrooms got their power and glow. Perhaps, it was a combination of the heat and humidity, the constant nearby electrical activity, or even a leaky sewage pipe. Regardless, none of them were in a hurry to notify authorities about the problem.

Now, once Bellocq had finished catching up with his crew and swigged a bottle of beer, he turned his attention to Megan. She had stirred some, but was apparently still unconscious. He leaned down and snapped off a piece of mushroom, popping it into his mouth.

While the mushroom itself had no flavor, each person reported an aroma unique to them. For Dylan, it was Roquefort. For Louis, a croque monsieur. That fucker Macron claimed it smelled like pussy. But for Bellocq, it was a mixture of vanilla and caramel, with a hint of orange.

"Come on, sweetheart, it's time to play," he told Megan as he moved toward her. When he was within a few feet, she bolted to her feet, took a few wobbly steps, then fell again. Just as she was standing again, Bellocq was upon her, grabbing a fistful of her hair.

"Now now, you mustn't leave yet. The party's just beginning." Bellocq licked her neck then, stepping back, swung Megan in an arc by her hair, slamming her into the side of the subway car, where she fell to the ground.

"Oh, my bad. I forgot that was there," he said with mock sing-song sarcasm. Bellocq laughed, and his crew joined in. Rubbing his hardened crotch with one hand, he lifted Megan with ease using the other. Two of his crew joined him and pinned her arms to the subway car.

A quick tug, and her t-shirt was in shreds on the ground. Bellocq looked at her white lace bra. "What, no front hooks? Going to make me work for it, are you?" He pulled a folded blade from his pocket, flicked it open, and slipped it under the front of Megan's bra, leaving a bloody trail up her chest. This didn't concern Bellocq, as he was focusing on her half-naked body.

"Well now, boys, doesn't that look yummy?" He pinched and twisted a nipple which hardened from the pain. "Oh, and it looks like she likes it rough. Just our luck."

Bellocq pocketed the blade, unfastened Megan's jeans, and pulled them and her panties to her ankles. As he stood, he licked her from between her legs to her chin, leaving a bloody streak on her upper chest and neck.

Tossing Megan over his shoulder, Bellocq grabbed her bag and went inside the subway car. He dumped the large bag on the floor, and a variety of cheap souvenirs spilled out. She was still stunned from being slammed into the subway car and didn't offer any resistance.

"What do you say, boys? Laying down or standing up?" Bellocq asked.

Louis grinned. "Oh, definitely standing up. Wouldn't want to get my jeans dirty."

Bellocq gave a sharp nod. "Standing up it is then." He gently lowered Megan so she was bent over the seat closest to the door, which folded up when not occupied. He then squatted and used her souvenir bag to tie Megan's wrists to her ankles. When he finished, he stepped back and admired his handiwork.

"Nice. Very nice indeed," Bellocq said as he lowered his jeans and underwear, exposing his erection.

Dylan tapped him on the shoulder. "Boss, this *salope* was cruising to get laid. You never know what kind of diseases she might have."

"Very true," Bellocq said while stroking himself. "Better use protection." He looked around at their belongings in the car before his eyes fell upon a metal Eiffel Tower he had dumped from Megan's souvenir bag. Picking it up, he slipped it over his penis. Arms spread wide, Bellocq grinned.

"Yes. I think this will work just fine."

☠ ☠ ☠

Two weeks later, Chloe spotted Bellocq as he guided another inebriated woman through the tunnels of Kléber. She watched as he arrived just after the last train left. The security monitors showed him sitting down with the short blonde leaning against him. After waiting for several minutes, his hand disappeared into his pocket, and the monitor filled with snow.

Chloe smiled. Now she had a face.

☠ ☠ ☠

It had taken another couple weeks, but Chloe had finally spotted Bellocq in the wild. She had seen him walking down Rue Lauriston, and when he stepped into Brasserie Seine, she followed, sitting at a table in the corner.

Saturday nights brought the biggest crowds, and it was the same night of the week Chloe had seen Bellocq with his victims. The crowd would make him and the women he targeted harder to remember, so it made sense to her.

She ordered only a carafe of water, earning a baleful glare from the waiter. But it served its purpose, as he didn't return, knowing she would not order much. This allowed Chloe to watch Bellocq operate.

It was obvious he had plenty of appeal to the ladies, but most of the women he talked to took the free drink he offered then moved along.

When the bar stool next to Bellocq was vacant again, Chloe moved quickly, leaving her glass and half-empty carafe of water. She leaned between him and the vacant stool, making sure her breasts rubbed against his arm.

"*Excusez-moi, cette place est-elle prise?*" she asked, intentionally making her French sound awkward and gestured to the empty spot.

"*Non, non,*" he replied with a dismissive wave, though Chloe noticed he stared at her cleavage as she got situated.

Though Chloe had lived in Paris for four years, her Mississippi accent always shone through when she talked. While she could speak passing French out of necessity, she also found it easy to slip back into her Aw-Shucks southern drawl.

"Pardon me, do you speak English?" she asked Bellocq.

He eyed her up and down then nodded. "*Oui,* some. I need more practice though."

"Oh good. I took French in high school, but that was years ago, and it don't sound nothing like what y'all speak it here." Chloe flushed and looked at her hands clasped in her lap.

"Can I buy you a drink?"

"Sure, but just white wine. I can't handle too much, so I have to keep to the tame stuff."

Bellocq ordered a glass of Moscato for each of them. "What is your name, lovely lady?"

"Savannah. It's also where I was born in Georgia." Chloe winked at him and broadened her grin, enhancing her dimples.

His head rocked back and he let loose a loud laugh. "Your parents named you after your city? Can you imagine anyone naming their child Paris?" Bellocq offered a curt "*Merci*" to the bartender as he accepted their drinks then returned his attention to Chloe.

"You don't much keep up with American celebrities, do you?" Chloe said and giggled.

"No, why?" An inquisitive look covered his face.

"Never mind. Thank you for the drink." She sipped from her glass. "Mm, nice and sweet, the way I like it. I just can't handle red wine. Way too bitter. This is much better."

Bellocq smiled and watched her sip. His glance moved around the room, as if checking to see if anyone had noticed him. "Would you like something to eat, Savannah?"

"No, I ate before I came over. I tell you, a McDonald's here is nothing like back home. Although they did have macaroons, so I ain't complaining." Chloe intentionally mispronounced the confection, hoping it would add to her charm. "But you go ahead if you want something."

He nodded and ordered a small charcuterie tray. They fell silent for a while, so Chloe moved as if to stand up. "I'll be heading out now," she said while gesturing to her half-full glass. "Thank you again for the drink."

"*Non, non, non*, please stay." Bellocq said while grabbing her arm. Chloe looked at his hand until he slowly removed it. "Please?" he added.

Chloe glanced at the door then her watch before finally sitting back down. "Okay then. I hate to waste a good drink bought by a gentleman." Bellocq beamed, and Chloe knew she had him.

They talked and laughed for a couple hours. Bellocq continued to buy Chloe wine, and she continued to sip at them while sneaking bites from the charcuterie tray. She wasn't hungry, but she loved salami and could never pass up a good brie or chèvre. As she drank, Chloe became louder and more flirtatious, touching Bellocq's arm or leg, putting her head on his shoulder briefly, and making her speech more stuttered.

But it was all an act. Starting in her mid-teens, Chloe had sneaked sips of homemade moonshine distilled by her best friend's grandfather. A sweet Moscato, compared to the rot-gut Chloe had cut her teeth on, was almost tap water. Or maybe near-beer at best.

As one a.m. approached, and she tired of the game, Chloe said, "I need to go to the little girls' room." When she stood, she swayed a bit, pleased when Bellocq reached out and stabilized her. "I guess I have reached my limit, kind sir," she added and giggled.

After carefully picking her way to the restroom, happy the brasserie wasn't one with a bathroom you had to pay for, an all-too-common situation in Paris, Chloe leaned against the sink and waited a few minutes. Before heading back to her bar stool, she carefully tucked the waistband of her skirt into the top of her panties, pulling up the hem to show thigh and just a hint of ass. She admired herself in the mirror.

"Perfect," Chloe assured herself.

☠ ☠ ☠

As his stumbling victim made her way back to her seat, Bellocq stood to greet her. "Excuse me," he said and helped adjust her skirt. He enjoyed the view, brief as it was, while doing so. His thoughts drifted to the mushrooms in the subway, the power and thrill they would give him, and he became aroused by the thought.

While he would take advantage of any shapely woman, Bellocq preferred blondes. And this woman, with her blond curls, blue eyes, and perky tits, was right up his alley. He and his crew were definitely getting lucky tonight.

"You were showing more than you wanted, I am sure."

"Maybe to everyone else here, but not you," Chloe replied and winked.

Bellocq's smile spread across his face. "It's very loud here. Why don't we go for a walk?" Chloe nodded. He shouted "*L'addition, s'il vous plaît*" to the bartender, settled his tab, and they headed toward the exit.

"Where are you staying, Savannah? I can help you get back home if you want."

Chloe stopped on the sidewalk and looked up and down the street. "Trocadero is the station I usually get off at," she said while pointing in the wrong direction. "I had taken the metro to the Arc du Triomphe and was going to walk back to my hotel." Her gaze fell on the front of Brasserie Seine. "But I got tired and had to stop."

"No problem, sweet lady," Bellocq said. "I'll get you where you need to be." He put an arm around Chloe, turned her, and they walked toward Kléber station, Chloe leaning against him slightly. End of the block, take a right, then another right, and they'd be at the station.

It took some effort for Bellocq to navigate her down the steps into the subway station, not that she was much help. He gladly used one of his own metro tickets for her and helped her through the turnstiles.

When Chloe stopped and squinted at the large signs for Nation, which would take her toward Trocadero, and Charles de Gaulle-Étoile, which would lead her in the opposite direction, confusion spread across her face.

"Shit, this is always so hard. Why can't they just list all the stations in each direction, rather than just the end points?" she asked while leaning her head against Bellocq's arm. "Being drunk doesn't help," she added with a giggle.

"I know. If I hadn't grown up here, it would be hard for me too. Here, let's go wait for your train," Bellocq said as he guided her down the tunnel toward Étoile.

"Thank you, kind sir," Chloe whispered then kissed his arm.

When they reached the platform, they sat in the uncomfortable plastic chairs and waited for the next train. Only two or three minutes separated the arrivals, so they wouldn't have long to wait. Chloe leaned against Bellocq and caressed his leg. As she did so, her cross-body purse slipped forward, hitting his leg.

"Here, let me take that for you," he offered, but Chloe shook her head and clutched it to her stomach. Bellocq thought that even though she was fading from the alcohol, her instinct to protect her purse must be strong. No worries. He'd have plenty of time to shed her of her belongings later. And her clothes.

The rumble of the approaching train announced its imminent arrival. Bellocq waited until it stopped then tried to stir her. "Come on, Savannah. We need to catch this train. It's the last one." He watched the smattering of passengers hustling into the cars. "If we miss this one, we will have to walk to Trocadero."

She moved to stand up, swayed, and sat down heavily. "Goodness, lady, you have had too much," Bellocq said with a chuckle. He helped her stand, but only after the tone announcing the closing of the car doors had sounded. By the time he got her standing, the doors were closed.

"*Merde*," Bellocq muttered as the subway accelerated away. "Well, you're in no condition to walk too far, pretty lady." He glanced around the platform, ensuring it was empty. "Let's sit for a moment to let you rest."

They sat back in the chairs for several minutes, Chloe resting against him. When he heard her breathing grow deep and shallow, Bellocq figured it was time to move.

His free hand slid into his pocket, and he pushed the button on the device. After waiting a moment to ensure it had disrupted the cameras, Bellocq guided Chloe to the lip of the platform. He helped her sit, but when he tried to lay her down, she resisted, so he left her alone.

Dropping to the ground by the tracks, he slid her off the platform where she landed chest to chest with him. "That felt good," she mumbled, but her eyes remained closed. Knowing she wouldn't allow it, rather than hoist her to his shoulders, Bellocq guided her toward his hideout. "This way, Savannah. Just be careful you don't trip."

Once they were fifty feet down the tunnel, he pressed the button again and continued their walk. A little further into the tunnel and Bellocq activated the flashlight app so he could guide them both.

As he steadied Chloe, he let one hand slide to her backside, which he grasped firmly. The anticipation of the fun he'd have with her made him smile. A little taste of those beautiful, glowing mushrooms, and he could bang on her for hours. He quickened their pace.

Dylan shouted a halt, as expected, as they approached the hideout. "Being a little lazy, boss?" he asked Bellocq. "Or is this one just too fat to carry?"

"She's had too many, but not enough that she can't walk." Bellocq cupped a hand under one of her breasts. "But she was definitely ready and willing, so I can't wait to get a taste of her."

"Us too, boss," his friend reminded him.

"Of course, of course. We have all night."

Bellocq walked Chloe behind the back subway car and leaned her against it. Satisfied she would continue standing, he went to the wall, grabbed a handful of mushrooms, and ate happily. Smiling and nodding, he gestured to Louis and Dylan to help themselves. It would be a night like no other.

☠ ☠ ☠

After letting Bellocq lean her against the subway car, Chloe listened as their footsteps receded. She risked opening her eyes slightly. There wasn't much light, just a faint blueish glow about fifteen feet away. She opened her eyes fully and watched as the three men reached to the base of the wall, picked something, and ate.

The three walked toward her and, since they caught with her eyes open, Chloe smiled at them. As the men got closer, she noticed their eyes glowing with the same lustrous color as whatever was on the wall. Bellocq stood before her, and it amazed her to see his shirt grow tighter as his muscles expanded.

"Hey, darling, is it playtime?" she cooed. A quick wink followed, which produced a smile from all three men.

Bellocq gestured to the men flanking him. "I hope you don't mind sharing, Savannah."

"Oh, honey, the more the merrier. It will probably take all three of you to take care of me anyway." She reached and caressed Bellocq's chest.

Chloe gestured for Bellocq to drop his pants, which he did. She stroked his erection and motioned for Dylan and Louis to also disrobe. For a couple minutes she took turns with them, making sure each one's focus was fully below their respective waists.

Dropping to her knees, Chloe took Bellocq into her mouth. To her left, she continued stroking Louis. Dylan, left out of the fun for the time being, was taking care of himself.

Chloe continued a little longer, ensuring all three were fully distracted by the possibilities of the night. Then she slipped a hand into her purse, which hung in front of her.

Snapping the four-inch blade from her purse, Chloe buried it to its guard behind Bellocq's scrotum as she spat him out. Withdrawing it slightly, she cut a deep C-shape groove into the inside of his thigh, severing his femoral artery in two places. Blood sprayed across Chloe's face and filled her mouth, but she didn't care.

Chloe shifted quickly to her left and, still holding Louis's erection firmly, removed it with a slash. As he doubled over, she stood and shoved the blade under his chin. Louis crumpled to a heap next to his boss, both spilling blood at a fatal rate.

She turned toward Dylan, who had stepped back a couple paces. The mushrooms prevented anything he might have seen from killing his arousal, but he didn't seem to care. His hands were high and wide, as if showing he didn't want any trouble.

"Don't let your dick run your life," Chloe told Dylan. He blinked a couple times in response, and his brow furrowed.

"What?"

"Don't. Let. Your. Dick. Run. Your. Life." She smiled at him. "Saw it in an old eighties movie. The title escapes me." Chloe waved her blade in the general direction of Dylan's penis. "But it's definitely good advice. Could you cover that thing, please?" she asked Dylan, and he quickly complied by pulling up his pants.

Chloe studied their surroundings. As she had dispatched the two men, the mushrooms' glow had intensified, as if pleased by the events. She could see better now and motioned Dylan toward the wall. He stood near her, but not too close, eyes wide and his crotch still bulging.

Reaching down, Chloe grabbed a piece of mushroom and eyed it closely. As she turned it over in her hands, the fragment pulsed more frequently.

At that moment, nothing could keep Chloe from taking a bite, the pull and enticement so strong, as if it were calling to her. She bit into it, and as she savored the chewy, fibrous texture, her nostrils filled with the scent of chocolate and bananas. She felt her muscles go taut, and her vision showed the tunnel as clear as if they were in broad daylight.

Chloe eyed Dylan, and her smile broadened. "I think I may just put you to good use after all." She shimmied out of her skirt and panties. Widening her stance, knife still in hand, she pointed at Dylan then between her legs. He quickly got to his knees and went to work.

Smiling with erotic pleasure, Chloe surveyed her new home. She would like it here just fine.

Author Notes

My Gorgeous Bride and I went to Paris in 2019 and fell in love with the city. There is so much about Paris that is fascinating, and not just the food, art, history, and architecture.

At one time, I remember reading about a stretch of the Paris metro station where abandoned subway cars were stored. It struck me as a great place for criminal types to hide out, being careful to avoid police, subway employees, and any lines that came through.

From there, it was just a matter of figuring out the elements of the story. Bellocq was actually named after a friend of mine who lives in Southern France, someone who has properly educated me on the difference between a *pan au chocolat* and *chocolatine*.

I'm not really sure where the inspiration for the mushrooms came from. Sometimes, those things just come out as you're writing, and you don't know from whence they came.

The details about the metro system, other than the mushrooms and criminals themselves, are true to what's in Paris, including the directions chosen, which stations are where, etc. As always, those little nuggets of reality add depth and believability to a story.

Tweets II

She dabbed at her rainbow of facial bruises, wounds of red, yellow, #purple, & black. Lip split by standing still. Fingers broken by blocking. Spirit dented but not broken. She grabbed his six-iron, stood where he hung, & broke open her piñata, her freedom spilling out. #vss365

☠ ☠ ☠

"Hear about ol' Jimmy?"

"Yep, bastard was killin' women, then hackin' 'em up & storin' 'em in his deep freeze."

"He ain't right in the head."

"Yep, his cheese done slid off his cracker."

"And I'm questionin' all them trips to the #Dairy Queens he owns too." #vss365

☠ ☠ ☠

My eyes lift from the #bottom of this pit, dug by your threats, denigration, & brutality, driving my soul to exile. Bruises, cuts, & fractures my reward for baring my heart. But my ladder out is built, constructed of support, kinship, & love, but especially your bones. #vss365

☠ ☠ ☠

A perfect #calm settled in the child as she realized what needed to be done. Getting dressed & kicking over the camera from its tripod, she bent a leg of the tripod back & forth until it broke, creating a ragged spear. Then she went to settle the score with her abuser. #vss365

Stumbling & swaying, he #swims through the pain. Breathe. In. Out. In. Out. Skin distended by the broken tibia, his next step pushes the bone through, needle through fleshy fabric. Nauseated and dizzy he falls, staring ahead as the headlights return to finish the job. #vss365

He eyed his restrained victim & pondered: 2-#cycle or 4-cycle chainsaw? The 2 was better for cutting through a femur, but the 4 was quieter & used less fuel. Unable to decide, he hefted his hacksaw, stuffed a shop rag in the man's mouth, & used good old manpower instead. #vss365

When Goldilocks woke, she found herself surrounded by three #bears sporting welcoming smiles. She was confused until she noticed the aroma of mesquite and saw the blazing grill outside. Then she finally realized these bears never liked porridge at all. #vss365

He missed the way she twirled her fingers in his #beard, pulling a little too hard, but he never fussed. He would just smile, tickle her tummy with his chin, listen to her giggle. Wiping a tear, he put a teddy bear on the tiny headstone, & began the long, rainy walk home. #vss365

☠☠☠

He walked to the side of the pool, feeling the #breeze blow through his hair & watching the families play. Laughing, splashing, dunking, all having so much fun. Shaking his head, he dropped the end of the extension cord into the water & walked away. "Damned kids." #vss365

☠☠☠

Dirt shoveled on me
Escape #impossible now
Eyes closed, I greet death

#vss365 #haiku

☠☠☠

Shorter than many stones around her, Clara cries on her knees, her love buried under the mound of dirt below. No money, no medicine, no insurance, no options, no Mommy, no #headstone. She is carried away by the social worker, already learning at two the cost of poverty. #vss365

☠☠☠

Coaching is important. Teach a child to #parrot what they should say. For their own good, of course. Erin walks into the house, & her grandma immediately notices the cuts & bruises on Erin's face & arms. "What happened, honey?" "Daddy said to say I fell off the swing." #vss365

☠☠☠

The sculptor set about her task, blade in hand. Nick here, tuck there, slice when necessary, even the occasional carve. Shape, mold, massage, trim, begin again. When #done, she admired her canvas of flesh, having finally formed him into the man she always wanted. #vss365

☠☠☠

Tim wasn't ashamed of the job. When you have bills & gambling debts to pay, any #capital was good. Anything to keep his joints bent the right way. Releasing a deep sigh, he eyed his mark through the windshield. Ignoring the Children Playing sign, Tim floored the accelerator. #vss365

☠☠☠

Susie had been taught to #obey, period, especially with Mommy gone. Daddy was always right, even when he crept into her room at night, sometimes with his friends. Now, as he lay drunk & naked, she slipped the knife from under the mattress & made him bleed down there too. #vss365

☠☠☠

Dan's world fractured when he saw Tami kissing another man. Now, hours later, she returns home to him, animated, smiling as if all is fine. He returns the smile, knowing she still loves him, & steps toward her from the #narrow ledge to her embrace six stories below. #vss365

☠☠☠

I was in love, but I #disappeared, heart folded like origami & placed in her pocket, to look at when she remembered it was there. Bent, frayed, tattered, & torn, she soon no longer recognized her possession & discarded it, just another shredded heart trodden under foot. #vss365

☠☠☠

Dummy. #Simpleton. Retard. Joe was tired of the insults. He eyed Cara & accelerated, feeling the satisfying bumps under his wheels. Popping the car in reverse, he slowly backed over her again, reveling in the glorious screams & crunches. One down. And the day was young. #vss365

☠☠☠

Thomas moves his #wiry frame forward pace by pace. One. Breathe. Two. Breathe. Three. Breathe. Four. Breathe. Five. He spins & holds the pistol against his thigh, refusing to raise it, just as the lead ball strikes him between the eyes, death & honor arriving together. #vss365

☠☠☠

Back & forth, back & forth, from wrist to elbow & back again. Sara's sawing with the dull blade only brought forth a few #measly droplets of crimson, but the pain was exquisite & freeing. Anything worth doing well took time. Gritting her teeth, she went back to work. #vss365

☠☠☠

The pundit who claimed the only #certainty in life was death & taxes never held their child as she took her last ragged breath, slipped away, & grew cold in your arms. A life half-lived with only half-certainty is a sorrow indeed. #vss365

☠☠☠

Gary watched his younger sister sleep & smiled. Nobody else was home, he had nothing to #lose, & he could be the first to make her bleed. Even at 12, she was nonverbal, so who would she tell?

He peeked at her blossoming form under the blanket & locked the bedroom door. #vss365

Antoine loves his job. Few understand the #relish he displays when duty calls. He always greets his client, silent though she may be. He smiles & encourages her to relax. Soon he opens his hands, lets gravity work, & the waiting basket gently cradles her falling head. #vss365

Emma bled. Cheeks, lips, legs. Even her panties were crimson when Daddy left her room. But he loved her. He said he did, so it was true. Words & actions conflicted in the mind of a battered child. But she chased no #opportunity for change. Because Daddy said he loved her. #vss365

Pam's smile that doesn't reach her eyes belies the trauma below the #surface, safely stashed under the chipper chatter & giggling. As Uncle Bob pats his lap & winks at the young girl, she sits without a word, despite his obvious arousal, lest Daddy call her a bad girl. #vss365

#Ecstacy fills Grace as she slides the blade across his chest. Circling a nipple with the tip, pushing just enough to draw blood, rivulets drip from his chest to join her virginal blood on the sheets. Zigzags down his stomach & a quick flick to ensure he'll rape no more. #vss365

Ally stood in the middle of her #trophy room, admiring its contents. A lock of hair here, two fingers there. An ear, a toe, even a few testicles. Men who tried to bed her succeeded, but all ended in the stew pot. After all, her freezer was too small to store all of them. #vss365

☠☠☠

Grace #sobs in front of the mirror, tears lost in the swirling sink. Daddy has used her yet again, six times this week, his cologne still heavy on her breast. Nobody believes her, even Mommy. Clutching the razor blade, she flexes her fist, finds the vein, & gets to work. #vss365

☠☠☠

Dana & Lana sit on the railing of their parents' sixth story condo. Legs swinging, enjoying the salty Florida breeze. A tinny tune wafts to them, & the twins spot an ice cream truck parked below. "Get me some ice cream, Lana." And with a #nudge, Dana is an only child. #vss365

☠☠☠

Billy charges through the #cavern, broadsword at the ready, until he reaches the throne room. The ogress towers over him, her haughty & demeaning visage staring him down. He lunges, severs her head, & stands triumphant over his abusive mother's corpse on the couch. #vss365

☠☠☠

The door closes, and with it the #Chapter of Our Lives, pages stained by the venom in your words, tattered by your infidelity. I stare at the blank slate in front of me, feeling only the emptiness there, knowing I'd rather you smudge me out than finish this book alone. #vss365

☠ ☠ ☠

Sally learned to #craft a good lie. Lies to avoid the bruises at home; lies to explain them at school. A means of survival transformed into an art form. Soon she knew not the true reality: what her Daddy told her, what she told herself, and what really was. #vss365

☠ ☠ ☠

We rise high above our nest, her talons a bloody #crown about my brow. Higher & higher, to rare air I've never known, our love a toxic potion of love & pain. I burn, I bleed, I cry, but she is near. I am content until dropped like an oyster on the jagged rocks far below. #vss365

Author Notes

There's not much specific to say about these, other than a note on some of the Southern slang and patois you see in some of my writing. I was raised and still live in Arkansas, so much of this is what I see and hear every day here.

Oh, and in compiling these stories and tweets, I noticed I apparently have a need to stage far too many stories on the sixth floor of a building.

"Second Fork to the Left"

The man hopped down from the top step of the wagon, grabbed his pack of belongings from the back, and spat on the ground. As the wagon rumbled off, stirring dust around him, he sauntered toward the nearest saloon. Two thirsts needed to be slaked, the first one wet and fiery.

Finding an empty table, the man took over an empty chair facing the door and placed his belongings between his boots. The place was mostly empty, the majority of the sparse patrons gathered around the faro table in the corner. Some were playing, others spectating while ribbing and goading the players.

"What can I get you, mister?" He shifted his gaze to find a young lady, not more than sixteen, beside him in a simple blue cotton dress. She was barely taller standing than him sitting. Her long blond hair had been tied into a simple ponytail, while some strands ran down the sides her face, having escaped their enclosure.

"Just a shot of rye, ma'am. And whatever snacks you got." The young lady nodded and left to fill the order.

While he waited, the man looked through the dirty windows of the saloon as best he could, trying to get a make on the town. Across from the saloon was a bank. On one side of that was a mercantile. But it was the building on the other side of the bank that caught the man's attention.

Standing outside of it were two young women, both in simple white cotton dresses. Between them stood one of the ugliest fellas the man had ever seen, but, based on the attentive women's hands upon his arms, back, and shoulders, he had enough money for them to overlook his physical appearance.

"Here's your drink, sir," the server said as she placed the shot glass and a plate of hard tack on the table. "That'll be two bits. No charge for the bread. You can pay at the bar if you like." Then she shuffled off to attend to the men around the faro table.

The man swallowed the rye in a single shot, wincing at its bite. No doubt, it had been cut with turpentine or some other nasty concoction to make the bottle go further. He tried unsuccessfully to bite into the bread, and, after banging it on the side of the table a few times, deemed it inedible before tossing it back onto the plate. Digging through a shirt pocket, he found four bits, tossed it on the table, then left the saloon.

He walked cattywampus across the way toward the brothel, careful to avoid horse and cow piles in the dusty street. When he reached the empty front step, he stomped his boots to free as much dust as possible from them then went inside.

The first thing he noticed was the huge man standing to the right of the door, arms crossed. The behemoth had to be at least six-and-a-half feet tall and probably had to turn sideways to get out the front door. His head was bald, either naturally or by choice, and a large, bushy mustache hid his mouth, the lengths of hair extending several inches beyond his chin on each side. A nod greeted the new guest, which was quickly returned.

"Greetings, sir, welcome to Bella's Place," came a soft, lilting voice with a Southern drawl. Through the swinging doors in front of the man came a tall, black-haired lady decked out in a long black, red, and white gown, the length of which barely covered her laced-up boots as she walked. The dress was adorned with white lace, as was the closed parasol she used as a walking stick. "I am Bella, of course. Please, have a seat."

"Thank you, ma'am, but I need to be going soon. If it's all the same to you, I'd like to get down to business soon." The man removed his hat as he spoke, his eyes on the madam's parasol, boots, the spittoon behind her, anything but her eyes.

Bella nodded. "I can understand that. Now, since you've not be here before, uh, Mister—"

"Jones."

"Very well, Mr. Jones. As I was saying, choosing one of our girls to spend some time with is a privilege reserved for our repeat customers. So, if you would kindly tell me what kind of lady you prefer, I can summon the best one for you."

The man's eyes continued to look at everything except Bella: the large framed paintings, sweeping staircases, vases, plus tables and trunks and chairs gilded with gold paint. "It might be rude, but can you tell me how much one of your girls is? I have money, but I don't like making deals without knowing how much it will cost me first."

"Not a problem, Mister *Jones*," Bella said, stressing the surname he'd given. "As a businesswoman myself, I always make sure I know what's at stake and what's to gain before entering into a contract. How else do you think I came to own most of the businesses on this side of the street, including the bank?"

For the first time, the man's gaze met Bella's, his wide eyes meeting her dark brown ones. He opened his mouth to speak, but finding nothing adequate or appropriate to say, closed it again.

"Whites are five dollars," Bella continued. "Blacks are three. We also have a Chinese and a Creek Indian, and each of them are seven."

The man pulled a coin purse from his bag, withdrew three dollar coins, and offered them to Bella. A giant hand appeared in front of him, palm up. All the man could do is stare at the massive hand, noting the beast blocked all sunlight from the window. For such a big man, he smelled of lilac and rose, which threw the guest off for a moment. Finally, he deposited the coins in the hand, which closed and moved away.

"Miss Emily?" Bella called then smiled at her customer. Soon a black woman who appeared to be in her fifties stood at the top of the steps. The white gown she wore stood in stark contrast to her skin, and the man noticed the years had not been kind to the whore's face, which was covered in wrinkled rivulets.

"Do you have anyone, you know, younger?"

Bella smiled and cocked her head slightly. "For three dollars, a first time guest, and my choice? No, sir. Miss Emily will take proper care of you, I promise."

97

The man nodded. "I will say, Miss Bella, that I have a tendency to like my play, shall we say, rough." His eyes avoided hers again. "I hope that will not be a problem."

"While bruises may not show as much on Miss Emily as they might on some of our fairer girls, they are indeed deterrents to future customers just the same." Bella glanced over her shoulder at her employee, who was still standing at the top of the steps, hands clasped in front of her. "Miss Emily can certainly accommodate you in whatever manner of business you wish to conduct, but we do ask that you return her to us in the same condition you found her, other than exhausted from doing her job."

"Yes, ma'am," he said simply, his eyes focused on Emily. "That I can do."

"Good, because if you do not, Mr. Stanley here will escort you outside, and I cannot promise he will use his gentlest manner."

After a nod of agreement from the man and a slight gesture from Bella's free hand, Emily descended the steps to greet her customer. The man noticed, as she approached, that her breasts swayed not bobbed. Still, he hoped she would do just fine for him.

Emily took the man's hand and slowly led him up the stairs. They proceeded to the end of the hallway, and as they went, several girls not already entertaining a customer watched them as they passed. Some smiled, some frowned, some appeared to be far away, perhaps in an opium dream.

Finally they reached her room, and Emily escorted him through the door then closed it behind them. "Would you like me to undress, or would you like to do it for me?" she asked.

"No, you can do it. I do enjoy watching that."

Emily smiled and pulled the white gown over her head, revealing her naked body. The man looked at the saggy breasts; stretch mark-lined belly that hung low, almost covering her thatch of hair; thick thighs rippled with creases. Even her face looked tired and worn.

"Have you had kids before?"

Emily squinted at the man a moment before answering. "Yes, sir. Four of them, all girls."

98

He nodded and stepped close to her. His hand touched her throat, and she lifted her chin in response. It then slid down her arm, over the wattle of flesh at the back of her upper arm, down to her wrist, feeling every wrinkle as he went. He paused for a moment, his thumb running back and forth in the valleys between the bones on the back of her hand.

The hand became a fist, the back of it striking hard against Emily's jaw. She grunted and fell backward, sitting on the edge of the bed. Her wide eyes stared at him, blood oozing from her lip and corner of her mouth. As she opened her mouth to say something, she barely had time to brace before another fist struck the side of her head. Then another. And another.

Emily's body was knocked to her side by the blows, crimson spattering the pillow, comforter, wall, and bedside lamp. As her arms flailed, searching, the man crawled onto the bed and straddled the prostitute. A barrage of punches found arms, face, ribs, chest, and a succession of crunching and snapping accompanied them.

Finally, Emily's hand found a rope and pulled it, managing to do so several times before her body went limp. The lack of resistance did not deter her attacker, and he continued to assault her, not noticing or caring about his bruised and bloodied knuckles, nor the red covering his shirt and vest and pants.

He continued striking the motionless whore until he felt something clamp around his neck and apply pressure against the back of his head. The man struggled for a few moments until all went dark.

☠ ☠ ☠

The man slowly opened his eyes, finding a large crowd of people in front of him, some blocked out by Stanley's massive form. It took the man a moment to realize the crowd didn't look right because they were sideways, and he sat up on the front porch of Bella's. His head swam and ached, and he had to put a hand down to steady himself.

"Mr. Jones, you disappoint me," said Bella as she stepped around Stanley. "Rules exist for a reason, and they are meant to be followed.

Otherwise, this would be a lawless town, not one people look for as a peaceful stop as they cross Indian territory from Fort Smith."

She adjusted the now-open parasol to block the sun then continued. "You are lucky Stanley here stopped choking you when you blacked out instead of depriving that brain of yours its precious blood." Bella gestured down the street with a dismissive gesture. "Otherwise, you would have been an unknowing customer down at Gabby's Coffin Company."

"I—" the man started, then decided he really didn't have anything to say in his defense. He'd agreed to what Miss Bella and Miss Emily were offering, and just because he didn't like it didn't mean he could break the agreement. In panic, his hands searched for his coin purse, finding it on the steps beside him.

"Yes, Mr. Jones, you still have your coins. They could have easily been 'lost' on your way down, what with Miss Emily needing some extensive care from Doc Rogers. You're just lucky she didn't need Gabby's services, or you'd be dancing from a noose by sunset."

The man opened his mouth to say something, but again finding no words that would serve his purpose, he closed it. He stuck the coin purse back in his bag. While he couldn't find his hat, he decided it would be best not to ask if he could go back inside to retrieve it. His eyes moved between Miss Bella and her mountain of a protector, waiting for them to give him instruction as he was obviously at their mercy.

Bella was the first to break the low murmur of discussion among the townspeople. "Since you have a very specific appetite that exceeds what we allow here at my fine establishment, I suggest you head on down the road west of here." The man looked in that direction and waited for her to continue.

"Take the first two left forks. After the second one, maybe thirty minutes ride from there, you'll see a house a couple hills off to the left. It's got an oak tree on either side of it, so it's easy to spot." The madam paused for a moment before continuing.

"There you'll find the Widow Reed. She's had a couple husbands since she moved out this way, and I hear tell a few before that. Word is that she dearly loves your type of entertainment and will meet you, so to speak, blow for blow."

"I—I don't have any way to get out there," the man managed.

"Well, you have boots, don't you? And based on the licking you gave Miss Emily, you're plenty strong too." Bella paused and looked around her, finding several nodding residents. "But I tell you what, I don't want you too tired for Widow Reed, so I'll let you borrow a horse from my stable near the end of town. Tell Bobby there that you want the old dapple. He'll take care of you."

The man waited to see if she had any more to add, and Bella added, "Get along now. We'll retrieve the horse later."

As the man stood and swayed, Stanley faked a step toward him and laughed when the stranger flinched, the humor not what the stranger expected from the giant. The man then gathered his bag and walked west toward the edge of town.

Just as Bella had indicated, Bobby gave him an old dapple mare to ride, offering nothing to the stranger but a wry smile, while also refusing payment. Then the man was on his way.

Along the ride, the man considered not stopping at all, to just keep riding to the next town. While the urge to get as far away from town as possible was potent, he knew he'd be labeled a horse thief if he didn't return the mare. So, after some contemplation, he decided to meet the Widow Reed, have some reciprocated fun, then return the horse and catch the first wagon or coach out of town.

The madam had given vague directions to his destination, so he didn't have any sense for how long it would take, but he found himself approaching the Widow Reed's house after only three hours or so on the trail. As he approached, a young woman in her twenties stepped out the front door, shotgun in hand.

"I'm looking for your momma, the Widow Reed," he called out to her.

The woman squinted at the stranger. "That's me. What are you doing out here off the road? We aren't too fond of strangers around here."

He looked at the rolling hills around him, where not another house could be spotted, and tried to figure out who "we" were. "I respect that. Miss Bella sent me."

Shotgun barrel now on her shoulder, the widow eyed him. "She did, did she? Why?"

"She said you had, er, similar tastes as mine." He felt uncomfortable talking about it with a woman he'd just met, unless they were soiled doves anyway. Miss Bella, sure. This widow? That was harder. The blood on his clothes would likely tell her more than he could anyway.

"Well, if she sent you, then I suspect I know why. And yes, it does get lonely out here, so I don't mind the occasional stranger stopping by for an overnight visit." The widow peered at the sun for a moment. "But it's a hard life out here. I only get by on what extra food I can grow and sell, or the odd pelts from wandering wolves. It'll cost you."

"How much?" The man braced himself for an exorbitant amount.

"Well, Miss Bella does alright with some of her exotic girls for seven dollars. So let's say ten."

He nodded, keeping to himself that he'd been willing to spend up to fifty if she was as equal to his appetites as reputed. "Fair enough."

"Toss the coins this way." He did as she instructed, then she gathered them up and dropped them into a pocket of her apron. "Draw some water from the pump for your horse, give her some, then tie her to the post over by that tree." The widow gestured to one side of the house. "You can feed her later. I know Bobby takes good care of his gals, so she'll be fine for a while."

Once the man had done that, the widow gestured for him to follow her into her house. The inside was a simple one-room affair with a kitchen table, cooking space, and bed. He figured that without any kids around, she must not have needed any privacy anyway. A peg by the door served as the place to hang a hat, and he started to remove his before remembering he'd left it in Miss Emily's room. So, he placed his bag below the hook, knowing it would be within sight of the bed.

"What's your name, mister?"

"Jones."

"No, it's not. I can tell when someone is lying to me. What's your name?" Her eyes narrowed as she challenged him.

"Jimmy Marshall. With two els."

"Alright then, Mr. Marshall with two els," she said as she gestured to a chair at the table. "Take your boots off and make yourself comfortable. You're gonna be here a while," she added with a wink.

"And you'll pardon me if I don't use your first name. Business is business, but I don't often have repeat customers. No sense getting personal, you know?"

Without a word, the man sat and removed his boots. While he did this, the widow poured some water into a basin and wet a cloth. Once he'd stood again, she removed his clothes in a business-like manner, no teasing, no playful banter, and washed him from brow to toe.

"I do have one rule, and that's no kissing on the mouth," the widow told him. "This is a business transaction, not a relationship."

"Understood," he replied, having no intention of doing so anyway.

The widow led him to the bed, where she removed her clothes slowly, but again in a business-like manner and nothing more. The coins in the apron pocket jingled when she dropped it to the floor, and Jimmy made a note to retrieve them later while she was sleeping. When she was done, she stood and let his eyes wander over her.

He stepped toward her and gently caressed her breasts, down her sides and legs, then finally to her buttocks. The man pulled her toward him then pushed her toward the bed.

"Let me take care of you first, Mr. Marshall with two els," Widow Reed whispered as she rubbed him to full attention. "Then you can do what you want with me."

"Yes, ma'am," he replied, knowing he could go again and again with no problem, so he might as well let her have her bit of fun before he could really let loose.

Widow Reed turned slowly, still in his grasp, and inched toward the edge of the bed. When he felt the mattress against the back of his thighs, he freed himself and sprawled on the bed, motioning her toward him with his hands.

"Happy to, stranger," she cooed and straddled him.

Immediately, Jimmy could tell she was aroused, and he adjusted his hips until their bodies were joined. She leaned forward, licked his ear, then left a trail of kisses down his chest before giving his nipple a quick nip with her teeth.

His body jerked from the unexpected pain, but it only served to further excite him, and he grasped her shoulders harder. The widow moved slowly to the other side of his chest and gave his other nipple the same treatment. This time, Jimmy was expecting it and reveled in the erotic sensation it gave him.

"Man, you do like it rough, ma'am."

"You have no idea," she said as she winked up at him from where her chin rested just below his. Then she sat straight up, grabbed his wrists, and fell forward, pinning them against the wall. Her tongue trailed up his chest to a bicep, where she bit hard, breaking skin slightly.

Jimmy jumped at the pain, having never received anything so intense from a woman before. But he knew his time was coming, then he would really show her what he was capable of. The gentle sound of her sucking at the new wound only further aroused him, and he grinned in anticipation.

Once again, Widow Reed worked a trail with her tongue and lips across his chest from one bicep to the other, where she clamped down with her teeth and ripped a mouthful of flesh and muscle from his bicep. Her face was instantly in front of his as she worked the meat in her mouth, blood spilling over her lips and chin to drip on his chest.

"Damn, woman, what the—" he said, then screamed the loudest of his life so far as the widow hooked both hands inside his elbows and jerked outward, separating both of his shoulders. Jimmy tried to lift his arms to push this hellcat off him, but even the slightest movement shot jolts of pain through his arms and chest. He bucked his hips, but found them pinned as if trapped under a mountain.

His head swam, but he finally managed to regain his focus, and he found the widow staring at him, still chewing slowly on her meal. As he squinted, she held both palms out to him, and long, curved talons grew from her fingertips. They dropped quickly to his chest, and he felt them dig into his flesh, each a fiery nail so strong he couldn't distinguish them. Then she dragged them down his chest, leaving crimson furrows in their wake.

Jimmy screamed again and once more tried to get the widow off him, to no avail. He remembered when he'd stepped into a gopher hole as a kid, trying to retrieve a stallion that'd broken out of the pen, and how he had used long slow breaths to control the pain in his ankle and regain focus. But this was worse. So much worse.

"Jimmy," the widow simply said, and he looked at her face again, a voice at the back of his head incongruously noting she'd used his first name.

Just as he met her eyes, the irises turned yellow, pupils reduced to pinpoints, and her cheekbones rose and sharpened. Her ears extended to points and her teeth transformed to a forest of fangs, the uppers extending below her lower lip.

The widow lifted her chin, arching her chest toward Jimmy, and he felt the bed began to vibrate. A loud screech escaped her lips as a pair of leathery, black wings extended fully, a loud snap filling the house as they did. They moved back and forth slowly, and he felt a slight breeze from them. Finally, she lowered her head and stared into Jimmy eyes, the yellow in hers almost shimmering.

"Almost done, mister." The voice that came from the widow's mouth was both deep, as if echoed from the deepest cave, while also as dry as the western desert.

Each thumb poked deep into his abdomen before finding purchase under his lowest rib, which she popped from his chest with a loud snap. The she moved to the next rib. And the next, slowly working his chest open.

Jimmy's mouth flew open, but no sound came out. He threw his head back and focused long enough to see the wall and headboard bejeweled with his own blood, dots and lines of ruby and garnet and cinnabar. Then the pain overwhelmed him and all was black.

☠☠☠

Some time later, Bobby rode up on his favorite Appaloosa gelding and untied the dapple mare from the post, fastening her reins to the back of his saddle. He stopped for a moment to watch the smoke rising from the widow's chimney, the sickly sweet smell accompanying it something he could never get used to. Then he turned his steed back toward town and left the Widow Reed alone with her latest meal.

✳ ✳ ✳

Author Notes

I had never written any weird western or horror western stories until I had a story published in the *Six Guns Straight From Hell 3* anthology. So when another call for a similar anthology came out, I decided to try the genre again.

This story wasn't accepted, but I've decided I really like the genre. In particular, these stories have given me some ideas for novel-length books, and those are already in the works.

"Swinging for the Fences"

The stench of her father's cologne clung to Amy's body, to her arms, legs, breasts. Everywhere. As she lay in her bed, arms hugging her legs, Amy bit hard on her knee, swallowing blood along with a scream.

This wasn't the first time her father had raped her. It wasn't even the first time this week. He had been doing it since Amy was eight, seven long years ago.

"I love you, baby," her father had said as he slipped a hand into Amy's panties. "And this is the special way daddies show love to their little girls." She had tensed and tried to scoot away from him, but he had held her down, kissed her on the forehead, and soothed her throughout.

"This is our little secret," he had told her every time he stole into her room. Amy had accepted his love because it was all she knew. He had taken care of her, buying her all the toys and games she wanted, reminding her all along how the gifts would disappear if his touch did.

So she had loved him back, learning to return affection in the ways he had taught her.

By the time she was eleven, Amy had grown numb to his touch, not giving a shit if he loved her or not. As she got older, she had graduated, as her daddy called it, from being violated by his fingers, to objects such as candles and screwdriver handles, to his dick. Amy had long ago learned to take care of him as quickly as possible, using her mouth or hips to sate him and get him out of her room.

When she was twelve, Amy had gathered up enough courage to talk to her mom about what was happening. "You little slut," her mom had spat, following the accusation with a hard backhand slap.

"You're just teasing him, aren't you? Making him want you, flaunting those little tits of yours around him?"

Another slap.

"This is your fault. You're taking advantage of Uncle James abusing your dad when he was a kid. Wiggle that ass in front of him, knowing he can't resist." Amy's mother raised her hand to strike her daughter again, but just shook her head and walked off. Amy never broached the subject again.

Not long after she turned thirteen, Amy had discovered a new sensation that only led to confusion: pleasure. Her body responded to his touch, and it felt good. This was so fucking against her will, yet she enjoyed it as much as when she touched herself. How could this be?

"Getting nice and wet now, aren't you?" her dad had said. A knowing leer appeared on his face, and he became rougher and more aggressive. "You want it, don't you, baby? See, I told you it was good for both of us." This newfound enthusiasm had led to him raping her more often.

That was also about the time Amy's dad had first flipped her to her belly and forced himself in by a new entry point. It had also flipped the switch in her from Indifference to Anger and Hatred, and it would never go back. She had hurt and bled for days.

Every time after that, she had fought back against him, kicking and punching and scratching. But he was so much stronger than her, and he would pin her with ease and do as he wished, which he did several times a week.

Amy started missing school, and whether she was hiding bruises or just didn't give a fuck about getting out of bed didn't really matter. She saw how everyone looked at her, and she felt them judging her for who she was and what she did. They knew. They had to know, right?

Amy's only refuge in life was softball, which she had played since she was six. Unfortunately, her dad was her coach, and despite being such a dick, he was a hell of a player and coach. But playing served as therapy of sorts for Amy as she could imagine each slug of a fastball being against her dad's skull. It wasn't much, but it kept her from imploding.

Now, as she lay on her bed, the hatred, disgust, and anger built in Amy. She rolled to the edge of the bed, letting her legs hang off the side. Noticing her panties still dangling from an ankle, Amy wiggled her foot, watching her underwear swing back and forth. *Bastard didn't even bother making sure they were off.*

Amy rotated her foot quickly, the panties spinning faster and faster, until a flick sent them flying into her bathroom, where they slid several feet across the tile floor. She sat and stared at them a while and tried to ignore the pain between her legs.

The blinking notification light on Amy's phone caught her eye, so she picked it up. Six missed calls, all from Erin, her best friend and softball teammate. Amy mustered all the strength and calm she could and called her friend back.

"Hey, E, what's up?"

"Amy, I—" Erin's voice cracked, and she started crying. "I—I don't know how to say this."

Amy shifted on her bed, pulling a throw across her naked body. "Just tell me, E."

More distant sobbing as if Erin had moved the phone away. Soon, Amy heard a deep breath followed by a slow exhalation. "Remember how I had the private lesson with your dad last night to work on my pitching?"

Immediately, Amy bolted upright. "Yes?"

"Well—" Another long pause. "After practice, I went to the bathroom to change out of my uniform. Your dad—" More silence, followed by a long sigh. "He said he would wait for me outside to make sure nobody else went in, but he followed me."

Knowing what was coming, Amy shook her head, not wanting to hear it.

"He bent me over the sink, pulled down my sweats, then pinned my arms with one hand and covered my mouth with the other. And—"

Her best friend didn't finish the sentence, but she didn't need to. *I can't believe it*, Amy thought. *The fucker did it. He raped Erin too.*

Amy didn't know what to say next, so she was silent. Eventually, Erin told her she needed to go and hung up.

Amy paced back and forth from her bedroom to bathroom, blood pressure, breathing, and anger all reaching a fever pitch. How many others had he raped? She tried to picture her teammates, thinking of any that might have a distant or pained look in their eyes, but she saw it in all of them. Amy didn't know if what she imagined was true, but she just couldn't help but think he'd raped everyone on her team.

Worse, she felt guilty for what had happened to Erin. Amy had told no one about her father, besides her mother. Maybe if she had told Erin before, they could have done something about it. At the least, Erin wouldn't have let herself be alone with him.

After grabbing clean panties, sweatpants, and a Here Come the Mummies t-shirt, Amy got dressed. She opened her door a slit and saw her dad where he usually was when not fucking her or making her suck his cock, on the couch with a bottle of Wild Turkey nearby.

Her mom had left a couple hours ago, supposedly shopping, but Amy knew she was probably out fucking some guy she'd met online or elsewhere. Now that she was older, Amy had figured out the truth about her father, that he was no longer turned on by her mother. It's a wonder they ever conceived Amy, but of course it only took one time.

Rather than have her mom bitch about Amy not doing her share of the chores, which really meant all of them, Amy headed toward her parents' bedroom to gather their laundry. As she crossed the living room, her father didn't acknowledge her presence, focused as he was on the Royals game on TV.

Grabbing the hampers of clothes and dumping them on her parents' bed, Amy sorted the clothes into piles of whites, colored, and towels. As she worked, she spotted a bottle of sleeping pills on her mother's side of the bed.

The longer Amy stared at the bottle, the more a plan developed. A plan to end the cycle once and for all.

On her way out of their bedroom with an armful of colored clothes, Amy slipped the bottle of pills into her pocket. She got the washer going, eliciting nothing from her dad but a mumbled, "Keep it down, I'm trying to watch the game."

Back in her room, Amy played Tori Amos on her laptop. She picked Tori because Amy loved her voice and lyrics, and the first song to play was "Silent All These Years". How appropriate.

She cleared off her desk and poured out a handful of pills. Using the top of her mouse, Amy rocked it back and forth, crushing the pills until they were a powder. Fishing an empty tampon wrapper from the trash can under her desk, she used her fingers to pinch tiny piles of powder into the plastic. Multiple times she had to resist the automatic urge to lick her fingers. Once she got as much of the powder into the wrapper as she could, Amy twisted the end of the gift package, folded it over, and placed it in her pocket.

Amy headed back to the living room where her dad was still planted on the couch. His bottle was almost empty, so she offered, "Want me to get some more Turkey for you?"

"The fuck you think?" he answered, not looking at her.

She grabbed the bottle from the floor by the couch and disappeared to the kitchen, glad to be out of his sight for a while. The cabinet beside the sink was where her dad kept his stash, and Amy retrieved a fresh bottle of bourbon.

After opening the bottle, Amy carefully poured her care package into the bottle. She wiped any powder from the bottle and counter top. Then she closed the bottle and shook it until she could see no more medicine.

Quietly Amy returned to the living room, placing the bottle on the floor by her father, the lid already loosened for him, as was her habit. Then she plopped onto the floor on the opposite side of the living room to watch baseball with him.

Over the next hour, Amy tried not to look at her father, lest it gather his attention. It was the heavy smell of bourbon that finally got her to peek in his direction. He was on the couch, eyes closed and chest rising and falling softly, the bottle of Wild Turkey on its side on the floor, spilling onto the carpet.

Amy waited a few more minutes before crawling over to her father. After setting the bottle upright, Amy poked him lightly in the leg, expecting an outburst from him. But nothing came. She poked harder and harder, but his eyes stayed closed.

As Amy stood, she smiled and looked down at her father. She disappeared to the garage where he kept his tools. After looking for a few minutes, she found his fifty-foot extension cord, which he used for outside Christmas lights.

Returning to the living room, Amy took one end of the cord and tied it between and around his ankles until she was satisfied with the series of knots. She tossed the other end of cord over the exposed ceiling joist, which took several attempts, and pulled the slack out of the cord.

Amy knew the joist would support her father's weight because he had demonstrated pull-ups from them several times. She wrapped the cord around her wrists and backed up, step by step, as her father's feet lifted into the air. Eventually, his whole body shifted as the motion moved him to the side, and the upper half of his body slipped off the couch and crashed to the floor. He didn't stir at all.

Emboldened by her success and father's lack of awareness of it, Amy pulled even harder, all the strength training for softball paying off. Soon, she was out of breath, but Amy kept pulling, inch by inch, until her father's feet were against the side of the joist. She tied off the extension cord on a doorknob and stood for several minutes, waiting to see if the cord would slip, but it held tight.

"Time to play," she said, a broad grin on her face.

Amy fetched an aluminum softball bat from her bedroom and analyzed her paternal piñata. "Where to start, where oh where," she muttered.

Standing beside him, Amy took a short, tentative chop, as if hitting a grounder in batting practice. She struck him on the side of his bicep, resulting in a light grunt and swing of the body, but nothing more.

"This could be fun." Amy tossed the bat into the air a couple times, catching it by the handle. She took a couple more shots at the side of his upper arm, each harder than the one before, and bruises began to sprout, a colorful and tangible reward for her efforts.

Moving to the other side of her father, Amy leaned her weight back, dropped her shoulders, and launched a swing, thinking fastball at the knees, and her bat made a satisfying connection with her father's lower arm. The arm shattered in the middle, and Amy watched with amusement as his arm swung both at the elbow and midway to the wrist. A louder groan escaped him, but his eyes stayed close. Neither fact registered with Amy.

She stood for a while, staring at a spot on his ribs near the armpit. "Power alley, baby," Amy whispered to nobody in particular. Measuring her distance, Amy reached her bat out until she was sure he was in the middle of her power stroke. Then she leaned back and let the bat fly.

His ribs caved on impact, the noise like someone stepping on a roll of bubble wrap. One rib poked through the skin, and a rivulet of blood worked its way the length of his arm, dripping from his fingertips to stain the carpet below him. A crimson line formed on the floor as his body swung back and forth.

Amy paced in circles around her father, contemplating where to hit next. She thought of Erin and what her father had done to her best friend. It only served to make her walk faster, narrow her eyes a little more, and breathe more quickly.

Finally, she stopped in front of him, readied her stance, and brought the bat down hard like an ax, the barrel landing solidly in his groin. The loudest grunt yet escaped her father, and his bladder released, urine mixed with blood running down his chest, most dripping to the floor while some settled in a nostril. Her father snorted and coughed, but his eyes remained closed.

Tiring of the game, Amy stared at her father's face, ready to end it for good. Again, she got into her stance and measured her distance. "Just like tee ball, baby," she chuckled.

Just as Amy had gauged the distance and brought the bat back, her father's eyes flitted open. It took a moment for him to focus on anything, his eyes still droopy from the drugs, but his gaze soon settled on his daughter. He shook his head slightly as if hoping to deter her.

She thought about all the years of softball, when she had swung with all her might, imagining her father's face on the ball.

Year after year of him holding her down with a hand across her mouth while he forced himself between her legs.

Repeated violent rape followed by professions of love.

"Sorry, fucker. You get to see this one coming."

Amy swung.

The barrel of her bat connected with her father's face on the upswing. His nose and orbital sockets collapsed under the impact. Teeth flew and scattered across the floor, one landing on Amy's foot. Her father's left eye shot out and swung across his forehead by the optic nerve. Blood poured to the floor, swamping any stains from her earlier swings.

Amy raised her bat to swing again but paused and lowered it to the floor. Her father was dead. No longer would he rape her or anyone else.

Seven years of pain and fear and anger and hatred had built in Amy, and they were finally free. She leaned against a wall and let the tears flow. The dam had burst, and she let it run its course, glad for the release. Soon the tears slowed, and Amy pulled herself together.

As she caught her breath, Amy heard the garage door open, her mother arriving home. She took a moment to brush a final tear from her cheek, wipe her bat clean on her father's shirt, then stood by the door to the garage.

Hearing keys jingle on the other side of the door, Amy shifted her weight back, lifted her bat high behind her shoulders, twisted her hips, and readied one final swing for the fences.

Author Notes

This story is another that was accepted for an anthology, but the anthology never materialized. So it reverted back to me to do with as I please.

By now, after reading the stories and tweets in this tome so far, you will know one of my common topics is victims of sexual assault obtaining their retribution. Of course, they don't always get that opportunity, but in this case, Amy does. Since the anthology was specifically about women and young ladies who break free from their abusers, this one fit right in.

Naturally, those who need their comeuppance aren't just the abusers themselves but those who know and let it go. In this case, Amy's mother was just as culpable.

As a side note, the Here Come The Mummies t-shirt referenced in this story is from a real band. They're a favorite of ours, and we've seen them many times. If you think you would like a band that does funk and jazz well, with lyrics littered with innuendo, check them out. You won't be disappointed.

Tweets III

You are The Gatekeeper of The Love #Dispensary, rationing affection, doling out hugs & kisses as you see fit. The rings we share should be an open prescription, but you choose to ignore it, closing the doors & barring the windows, unless some other patient should call. #vss365

☠☠☠

I toss the match & it ignites the gasoline-soaked wood siding of our house. Just like that, our home is in flames, one Susie & I kept through our marriage, raising children, & traveling the #globe. As I walk away, I can't help but wonder if I should have woken her first. #vss365

☠☠☠

Deb glares at the drunken, sleeping form of her rapist. Hatred & anger fill her, a desire to force him to share her #misery consumes her. But she dresses quietly & takes the DNA evidence between her legs & under her fingernails to the ER for the best possible punishment. #vss365

☠☠☠

I buried my sister in the field behind our house. The frozen ground couldn't be turned so I laid her to rest above it. All that remains is a cairn of memories, her name etched on a rock with a

#pen. Now back to the house with a hammer & hatred to even the score with Dad. #vss365

☠☠☠

Gail & Robyn pulled harder on the #rope, leaning away, pulling again. Perfect. They tied it off on the porch railing & went to admire their handiwork. Cousin Dan kicked & flopped, fingers trapped under the noose around his neck, but he'd touch the young girls no more. #vss365

☠☠☠

Tony curls up with Mommy, both of them naked. He is 13, but she is his #sanctuary, his safety net, his normal. His friends don't understand, so he talks to them no more. Mommy said it was for the best, & she always makes him feel warm, especially with her special cuddles. #vss365

☠☠☠

The #longing intense, I follow its pull. It takes me, as it always does, to the field of memories, one shared with many others. I stare down at the stone, the bookend dates only 12 years apart. Home is indeed where the heart is, even if it's six feet under ground. #vss365

☠☠☠

Our exchange of rings started the story of our life, but I was to be a #nobody, a cameo, an NPC. Through the years she auditioned many others, ever vigilant to be the star. I stand over her sleeping form, scarf taut between my fists, & bring the curtain down. #TalesNoir #vss365

☠☠☠

Ben relished his meal, from succulent flesh to the #crisp snap of bone & sucking of buttery marrow. He picked his teeth with an ulna fragment & pondered. Now that his children were gone, the freezer was empty. Laughter from the adjacent park shook him from his reverie. #vss365

☠ ☠ ☠

Dave stared at his baby, with those oddly-shaped eyes & perpetual smile. He was their first born, a son, but Dave was still unhappy. The baby was everything, plus an extra chromosome. Dave grabbed the pillow & pressed hard, giving all of them the #comfort they deserved. #vss365

☠ ☠ ☠

Years of abuse lead to a #slow Soul Death, but the body lives on. Bloody lips, bruises, vacant eyes, random missed days of school, they become your norm. First chance you get, you find "love", break away, start over. And the cycle lives on in your own broken children. #vss365

☠ ☠ ☠

Side by side we sit, tossing barbs & cuts & venom at each other until nothing remains of our #past but a #molten river of hatred & regret. There was a day when you cooled my fire, but now you stoke it, fanning the coals & feeding the flame until I am but ash & char. #vss365 #Syn7

☠ ☠ ☠

Eying her sleeping husband, Mary bows her head, the good subservient wife. All she could offer was a dowry of flesh and first blood; all she received in return was a #solitary life of neglect. Thrice this week she left the gas stove on. Tonight she lights that match. #vss365

☠☠☠

Christmas tree shines and sparkles, family laughing & hugging. The children chatter as they tear into presents. You love them, but how can you #enjoy the day when your own child is dancing in heaven? You know she's in a better place, but you'd rather she be in your arms. #vss365

☠☠☠

You lounge upon your Throne of Pain & #indulge my existence with a dismissive & haughty laugh. I climb upon a pedestal to straight-en your crown, hoping to gain favor, but you kick my perch from beneath me. As I tumble & bruise & break, you reward me with an "I Love You". #vss365

☠☠☠

Ann holds The Child close, the one with the absent voice & crooked limbs. Wrapped in a blanket, It is held closer, tighter, until It moves no more. She places It in the ground, wrapped in Its chrysalis, hoping for a new #beginning, transformation, & wings to soar On High. #vss365

☠☠☠

The itch is born as a murmur deep inside me. It blossoms & festers & calls to me, demanding freedom. Within reach, a pencil. A hard stab & my work begins. Fingers dig & pull & tear until the blue worm of my entrails, & with it the itch, are released from their #cage. #vss365

It won't shut up. That damned baby. I feed it, change it, rock it. Still, the racket, it just won't stop. I #slide the needle into my arm, smile, push the plunger, & wait. My own special blend of heroin & Drano will finally bring me blessed silence. #vss365

☠ ☠ ☠

The children dig into their meal of fried potatoes, brown beans, & Johnny #cakes. Our oldest stops mid-chew & looks me in the eye. "Mommy, aren't you & Daddy eating?" "No, we're not feeling well." Jimmy, wise beyond his 7 years, pushes his plate away too, saving the food. #vss365

☠ ☠ ☠

Dave's son always wanted to be #chef, before depression devoured him slowly from the inside out, the last thing he ate being a .45. The same demons now claim Dave, as he takes his son's santoku & fillets his forearm in nice neat rows of crimson, pain, & regret. #vss365

☠ ☠ ☠

Stepping out of my car with an armload of Christmas gifts, I gawk at the tar-paper house, little more than a shotgun #lean-to. Inside, a mini-fridge, single-burner stove, empty cabinets, & six pillows in the single room stun me. At home, I push away my full plate & cry. #vss365

☠ ☠ ☠

My wife, she makes angels. I've seen it with my own eyes. Three times she has held our beautiful newborn babies, with their tiny #pink knitted hats. And three times I've watched them grow still, sprout their wings, and fly away. #vss365

☠☠☠

I remember when we found Momma floatin' face down in the #pool. Katie was four, & I was five. I went inside & got some sweet tea, knowin' Momma'd be thirsty when she was done swimmin'. We got hungry & fixed sandwiches, but it was days 'fore anyone came to check on Momma. #vss365

☠☠☠

I caress your face with my hands, my fingers tracing every curve & angle. I must #read & memorize your face now that I can no longer see it. At least I will no longer cast my eyes upon another woman, now that you've removed my sight using my favorite drill. #vss365

☠☠☠

As I pull her #close, I feel her stiffen, a sudden distance appearing in her haunted eyes. I whisper soothing words, caress her back, kiss her tenderly. I know she's #closing me off, & I hate him for her fractured trust & shredded heart. Hurt is instant, healing forever. #vss365

☠☠☠

The final treatment was today. My choice. Pain is my constant companion since The Big C came to town, & the only #escape is hand-in-hand with The Man With The Scythe. I press the barrel to my temple, invite him in with a squeeze, & he arrives as the hammer strikes. #vss365

☠☠☠

The placid surface of our love was shattered by our baby's death. We tried to #overlook the impending tsunami, but it was not to be stemmed. Slamming into us, we caught its full brunt, the waves tossing & dividing us until we drowned, along with our marriage, alone & cold. #vss365

☠☠☠

I cower on the couch as she hurls another plate at me, shattering against & slicing my elbow. Her eyes shroud me in a #robe of contempt. The cuts from her hate run deep, but my love runs deeper, an infinite well that cannot be staunched by blood or pain, only death. #vss365

☠☠☠

She insists we're not over. I hear her words, but I don't feel them, not in her absent tears, her feigned #vehemence, or her vacant, emotionless eyes. I know we're tipping on two wheels at high speed, a crash imminent. And when I return from work, she will be gone. #vss365

☠☠☠

I's never fond of th' root #cellar. But we tore to it as th' twister bore down. Doors bolted from th' inside, only candle f' light, I's thigh deep in water from th' leaky walls. I's fine 'til I felt th' brush o' scales again' m' ankles & fangs buried in th' meat o' m' calf. #vss365

☠☠☠

Min swings the driver like her hero, Pak Se-Ri, visualizing the ball sailing down the fairway to the green. Rolling up her pants like Pak in the pond, cuts & bruises now visible, Min swings again, driver head spattering her #olivine walls black with her husband's blood. #vss365

☠☠☠

Peppermint, #butterscotch, or strawberry? Ellie loved the red & white stripes, but she loved yellow even more. Shedding a piece of its wrapper, Ellie popped it in her mouth & swallowed. By the time Daddy noticed, Ellie's flesh was the color of her Cookie Monster jammies. #vss365

Author Notes

As with most of the included tweets, there's not so much a specific inspiration as the first thing that came to mind when considering the word of the day. Of course, there are recurring themes, namely that we don't always need supernatural monsters when there are plenty of human ones who walk among us.

"Must Go Back"

The alarm on my phone startled me awake at two a.m. We'd only gotten a couple hours of sleep, and I had to resist the urge to push "Dismiss" and roll back over to let the Sandman claim me for the rest of the night.

But this was a big day, one my son Robert and I had been looking forward to for months. We were finally going to climb to the summit of El Pico Duarte, the highest point not just here in the Dominican Republic, but in all the Caribbean. Robert and I had hiked all over the Rockies, Appalachians, and had even tackled the Tour de Mont Blanc through the Alps and the Inca Trail through the Andes.

While we loved challenging ourselves vertically and physically and were looking forward to conquering El Pico Duarte, my wife and daughter-in-law were soaking up vitamin D on the beaches of Bávaro. That was fine with us. We all worshiped nature in our own ways.

I shook Robert awake, and he blinked at me, rubbed his eyes, then nodded, rolling from his side of the bed and stumbling to the hotel bathroom. As he showered and dressed, I checked our packs for the essentials we would need for our trek: blanket rolls, heavy gloves and stocking caps, a variety of carb- and protein-laden snacks, clean socks and underwear, battery packs to charge our phones, and other necessities. The guides we had hired were providing a tent for us to use, so at least we didn't have to lug that from the States.

They were also providing a mule, not only for packing supplies, but giving us brief respites from hiking. Based on our climbing experience, we didn't believe we would need to ride the mule, but the company hiring the guides on our behalf insisted. We were already paying three hundred and fifty dollars each for this excursion, so the additional fifty for the mule hardly seemed to make much difference. So what the hell.

In the lobby, we were greeted by two men, both lean and muscular. The older stepped toward me and gave my hand a vigorous shake. "Señor Jensen, no?"

"Yes, I am," I replied, the handshake setting my arm and shoulder in motion. "But please, call me Terry. And this is my son Robert." The man side-stepped quickly and gave Robert the same vibrant greeting.

"I am Pepe. And this is my youngest son, Gordo," the man said after finally granting Robert's hand freedom.

Both men had the look of experienced, athletic guides. Their frames were almost identical, the key differences being Pepe's hair, which had faint salt-and-pepper highlights among the black, and their eyes. While Pepe's eyes were wide and animated, Gordo's were half-closed, giving him a sleepy appearance.

"Come, we must hurry, *señores*, if we are to get to the trail in time," Pepe said as he grabbed my pack and Gordo took Robert's. "We have several hours to drive to get to the park entrance."

We rode in the back of a small pickup, maybe a Toyota or Nissan. I couldn't tell because it had no tailgate, a series of bungee cords across the back of the bed all that kept us and our supplies from bouncing into the road. Gordo rode with us, giving us the place of honor near the cab while he sprawled close to the opening in the bed. Every bump we hit jounced us, and I expected Gordo to roll out, but he had obviously done this many times and adeptly adjusted his balance.

It was late January, not the time of year most people would think to go mountain climbing, but in the Dominican Republic, their winters rarely saw temperatures below sixty-five Fahrenheit. The peak of El Pico Duarte was over 10,000 feet above sea level, so it would be plenty cold there, thus the need for shelter and blankets. While Marie, my wife, and Hailey could sleep with their doors open at night, enjoying the seventy degree weather, Robert and I would be bundled up trying to stay warm.

More important to the success of our climb, winter months were less rainy, so the trails up the mountain wouldn't be a sloppy, muddy mess. Still, it would take us three days to make the round trip. I can only imagine how long it would take during the rainy season, if people would even go at all.

Just before dawn, we arrived at the entrance to the national park. Robert and I unfolded ourselves from the bed of the truck and stretched our cold, stiff muscles. Gordo hopped over the side of the bed and made his way to a man holding a mule by a rope. The men exchanged some bills, and we had the final member of our climbing party.

As our guides loaded the mule with gear and supplies, both ours and theirs, I asked, "Does the mule have a name?"

Pepe and Gordo exchanged glances and shrugs before Pepe offered "Mulo?" Well, that made sense. I asked no more questions about the beast, and we were soon ready to begin our ascent.

The sky was clear, and we were far from any cities, so the nearly-full moon was as clear as I'd seen in a long time. I had intentionally picked this time of month to climb, believing the brightness of the moon would help guide us at night. While we had about ten hours of hiking to do today, we would only get a few hours of sleep before rising at three a.m. But that last few hours' climb should get us to the summit of El Pico Duarte just before sunrise, giving us a magnificent view and photo opportunity.

That was, if the clouds were not too low tomorrow morning. It would be a shame to make the trek only to have an obstructed view of the sunrise, but that was one thing you had to accept if you were going to climb like we did: Mother Nature was a fickle creature, and her mind was her own.

Day one was long but mostly uneventful. We managed to cover about twelve miles, climbing from the trailhead at La Cienaga to the typical overnight stopping point at La Compartición. It was a gradual ascent with no steep inclines to speak of. Some of the trails were narrow, and I worried about the mule's footing. But he managed it all with an almost bored air, stepping where needed as if he'd made the journey a hundred times. And he probably had.

Along the way, we saw several crystal-clear streams, filling our water bottles as needed, while also throwing in a purification tablet, just in case. Fortunately, narrow bridges had been laid across the water we had to cross. They looked old and rickety, but managed to hold a person or two at a time. At each one of these crossings, either Pepe or Gordo would lead Mulo through the stream, often getting soaked to their knees. I didn't envy them, but neither did I offer to do it instead.

Not only did we see stunning trees and plants, there were many birds that flew across our path or chattered from branches above us. I was tempted to stop and take pictures, but we wanted to keep a steady pace, so our hands stayed firmly attached to our climbing poles, and we continued.

Through much of the day's journey, a single crow followed us, alighting ahead of us and cawing, then once we passed, it would circle above or around us before landing ahead of us again. Several times our guides tried to shoo the bird away, even though it wasn't bothering us, but it persisted. It finally disappeared just before we stopped for the night.

At La Compartición, Robert and I checked out the cabin built there, looking forward to a warm night when we noticed the chimney, but after spotting several rats inside, we decided the tent wouldn't be so bad after all. Gordo set up our tent near the treeline, and we stowed our gear and blankets inside. Pepe got a blaze going in the provided fire ring and heated some asopao, a traditional Dominican stew, ladling a bowlful for each of us. Well, not the mule; he had grain.

The asopao was wonderful. While at the beachside resort, we tended to stick to known foods at the buffet, so this was the first chance we'd had to try traditional Dominican cuisine. The combination of chicken, vegetables, and fragrant spices, which had obviously been slow-cooked, were a mouth-watering combination, and we all ate heartily.

Wiping his mouth with the back of his hand, Pepe gestured with his spoon to the empty campground around us. "It is unusual, not having more here," he said before taking another bite. "Maybe it is because it is not the weekend. More on Saturday, Sunday for sure."

"Pepe," Robert asked, "why did you two keep trying to chase the bird away earlier?"

The old man finished his mouthful then paused. "They are supposed to be bad—" He searched for the right English word. "Bad things happen."

"A bad omen?" Robert offered.

"Yes, the *cao* is a bad omen. It means bad things will happen. So we chase it away."

We ate the remainder of our meal in silence, and I took the opportunity to study Pepe. While he was older and smaller than me, he somehow looked more physically fit, even though hardly a day went by that I didn't exercise. A glance at his forearms showed tight cords of muscle, honed by years of work, the calluses on his fingers and palms reinforcing this.

Near the clearing where we camped was a stream, and our guides encouraged us to bathe in the chilly waters. Since there was nobody around to embarrass with our stunning physiques, at least that's what we told ourselves, Robert and I stripped naked to swim and wash. I was a little worried a fish or some other wildlife in the stream would decide it needed to latch onto my gonads, but as cold as the water was, there was no concern. My manly pride practically retreated inside my body seeking warmth.

Once we were dry and dressed again, Robert and I joined our guides around the campfire. With the sun down, the temperature was dropping quickly. I didn't know how cold it was, but I knew I would be thankful for our thick sleeping bags and blankets.

Gordo had washed and stowed our dishes while we bathed, and he now inverted the largest bowl and played it as an impromptu drum. Robert closed his eyes and swayed with the rhythm, but I noticed Pepe was studying the air and trees around us.

"Is everything okay, Pepe?"

He looked at me briefly then gestured to the edge of the clearing. "The clouds are low. Too low. It will make the climb tomorrow very hard." His gaze met mine and held it. "We should go back. It won't be safe. Maybe the *cao* was warning us."

I nodded. "I understand, but we have climbed higher peaks in much heavier fog. We had to stop when we were in the Andes, maybe for six hours or so, waiting for it to pass."

It dawned on me I may have misjudged the old man, and perhaps he was trying to coax more money out of us. That was fine, I didn't mind. Most locals when I traveled preferred to negotiate and adjust rates. "If you are worried about getting hurt, we can pay more."

Pepe looked down and spat into the campfire. "I will give back half of our pay if we go back now. It could be very dangerous." His eyes stayed fixed on the fire.

"I appreciate that, but I really want to finish this climb. We leave the day after we get back, so we really can't afford any delays."

"Okay then," Pepe added in a whisper. "We must leave earlier though."

Worn from the climb, exercise, and bountiful meal, not to mention Gordo's soothing percussion, I soon found myself dozing. Excusing myself from the group, I made my way to the tent, triple-checking the alarm on my phone before plugging it into the battery pack, and climbing into my sleeping bag. Anticipation flooded me as I thought about the short three-mile climb to the peak awaiting us in the morning, tempered by Pepe's warning, but it wasn't enough to keep me awake, and I was soon asleep.

I never knew when Robert joined me, but he was in the adjacent sleeping bag when our alarms went off at three a.m. We crawled out of the tent, and I have to say I wasn't surprised to find Pepe and Gordo already awake. Mulo had already been packed with their gear, causing him to lean somewhat to the right. Seeing they were ready to go, we hurried to the tree line to answer nature's call then packed and loaded our side of Mulo.

It was colder than when I had gone to bed, since it was the middle of the night. Pepe pointed in the direction of El Pico Duarte, though we couldn't see it because of the surrounding clouds, which almost obscured our vision. "It is still very hard to see. Are you sure you want to go up?" he asked, shifting his gaze between my son and me.

"Absolutely," Robert said almost immediately. I nodded agreement, not wanting to be deterred.

We began our final ascent with Pepe in the lead and Gordo trailing. Because it was dark with no moonlight, and the climb would be the steepest of the entire trek, we had to pick our steps slowly and carefully. The older man asked me to guide the mule, and Robert followed behind me.

According to our guides, the final push would take us about two hours under optimal circumstances. With the clouds low, obscuring our view, it would definitely take longer. But Pepe assured us, with a sharpness in his tone, we'd be able to get our selfie with the bust of Juan Pablo Duarte at the summit, all while taking in the gorgeous sunrise.

While Robert had the foresight to pack flashlights for our night travels, our guides were even more prepared. They had given each of us headlamps we could wear over our stocking caps, and that made much more sense than trying to hold a flashlight while both hands were busy with hiking poles, or in my case, Mulo's rope.

Much of the trail was narrow, with a wall of dirt on one side and a steep drop-off on the other. Gordo instructed me to make sure I walked with Mulo between myself and the edge. It would be difficult to lose our ride and gear, but at least it wasn't as problematic as me taking a plunge down the mountainside.

As we climbed, the fog seemed to thicken, and I presumed we were going through the heaviest part of the clouds. It made for slow progress, but I was hopeful the lower cloud cover would mean we'd be above it when we reached the summit. It drove me on, anticipation rising with each step.

About thirty minutes into our morning journey, we heard a cacophony of birds above us. I stopped to look about, and Robert, his head down watching his steps, bumped into Mulo's hind end. The beast was not amused and swished his tail in annoyance at my son.

I looked above us, and several crows circled, swooping low then disappearing into the fog before flashing into view again. Pepe mumbled something in Spanish under his breath and continued up the path.

We climbed for several more minutes, then, as if flipping a switch, the crows were immediately silent. Pepe halted and held up a hand for me to stop. The man glanced backward with a furrowed brow at his son, who shrugged and said nothing.

As I waited for our guides to continue, I was assaulted by the heavy miasma of decay. Since I had grown up on a farm, I had been around countless animals in various stages of decomposition, and this stench reminded me of that odor. But this seemed like we were in the very midst of it, as if the trail itself was made of rotted flesh. I pressed my nose into the crook of my elbow.

"What is that stench?" I asked Pepe.

The man chewed on his lower lip as if pondering, then answered, "Mule, I think." He pointed down the hillside into the darkness. "Sometimes they slip, mostly when the trail is wet." Pepe held my gaze for a moment, then looked down again.

"It could also be men. They fall sometimes too." He paused and took a deep breath, letting it out slowly. "I have lost two before." I wondered if he meant mules or men but decided not to ask.

"But the trail isn't wet. It's been pretty dry," I offered. Behind me, Robert made a retching noise. I turned and looked at him, but he waved me off.

"True. But bad luck happens," Pepe added then started walking again. "Come, since you insist, we must finish the journey and make our way down in the daylight."

I started after Pepe, but the lead tied to Mulo soon grew taut, making me turn back to him. His weight was shifted toward Robert, and his ears were laid back, as if pointing back down the trail to home. I pulled on the rope a couple more times, but the mule refused to budge. Their reputation for stubbornness was well-earned.

Robert raised his hand as if to swat the mule's rump, but Gordo quickly grabbed his wrist. "No. He will kick," the younger guide warned. My son nodded and lowered his arm.

Moving closer to our beast of burden, I grabbed his halter with my hand and tugged with all my strength. The animal resisted for a moment then lurched forward with a start. I suddenly found myself on the wrong side of the trail, with nothing but air behind me as the mule bumped into me with his shoulder.

Out of instinct, I stepped backward, but my left foot found nowhere to rest, and I fell. Just as my right foot began to slip off the trail, Mulo stepped on the foot, pinning it to the dirt. A loud pop resonated from my right knee, and I screamed in agony.

Fortunately, the mule stopped for a moment, perhaps to see what had caused the racket, before continuing up the trail after Pepe, and that pause allowed Robert to grab my arm. Gordo wrapped an arm around Robert's waist and pulled. The impromptu human chain worked to prevent my further descent, and they pulled me back onto the trail.

As I lay on the dirt and rocks, breathing heavily and limbs shaking from the adrenaline rush, I heard Pepe come back toward us. He muttered something sharp in Spanish to the mule as he passed then squatted beside me.

"Are you good, Señor Terry?" he asked. I kept my eyes squeezed shut and shook my head. "Where does it hurt?" Pepe continued.

I leaned to my right while on my back and tapped just above my right knee. "I felt it pop." Robert knelt beside me and gently probed around my knee. I winced as he poked and squeezed.

"Do you think you can stand, Dad?"

"I can try, but I'll need some help getting up." I lifted my injured leg off the ground and offered my hands to the young men. They pulled, and I was soon wobbling on one leg. It only took a moment of putting weight on my injured leg to know I would be unable to walk. I shook my head and leaned against Robert.

"We need to go back down," Pepe offered. "You need a doctor."

"Hell no," I shot back. "We're this close. I can ride that damned mule." We all turned to look at the animal, who stood about fifteen feet from us, looking back over his shoulder. His ears were forward as if listening to our plans.

"*Señor*, I really think we need to go back. You can make the trip again next year when you are healed. The signs are telling us we should stop." He gestured vaguely around him. "The *cao*, the clouds, you getting hurt. All bad signs. We should go back."

"How much longer do we have?" Robert asked. He had been on so many climbs with me, I had no doubt he was aware of my refusal to quit anything I had started.

Pepe looked at Gordo, who only shrugged, as usual. The older man let out of long, exasperated sigh. "Maybe two hours, maybe a little more. If you ride the mule, we can go a little faster than we were before."

I ignored the dig at my walking speed. "Fine. Get that beast over here."

The trail was too narrow to turn Mulo around, so I wrapped an arm around Robert and Gordo, and they helped me hop to where my ride waited. After moving the animal's load closer to his haunches, they lifted me so I lay on my belly over the animal, and with some assistance, I swung my good leg over him. I slowed my breathing, trying to ignore the burning in my knee, and finally nodded. "Let's go."

We continued our climb, Pepe and Robert ahead of Mulo and me, Gordo bringing up the rear. I tried to sit upright on the mule, but the pain fatigued me quickly, and I soon found myself leaning forward, my arms wrapped around the animal's neck. As we climbed, the rocking lull of Mulo's motion almost put me to sleep, but the jarring in my injured leg and resulting pain woke me every time I got close.

Some time later, Pepe stopped suddenly, and I heard him hiss for Gordo. I lifted my head and saw him motion to his son. The younger man passed me, and the other three stood in a semicircle, looking at something in the dirt.

"What are they?" prompted Robert.

Pepe looked up the bank of dirt where a patch of pine trees was scattered, then down the steep hillside. The man crossed his index fingers as if making an X or a cross and displayed it back and forth to the darkness below us. Then he looked back at the trail, shook his head, and exhaled slowly.

"*Ciguapa*," he pronounced, and Gordo made a quick sign of the cross on his body.

Guapa? I thought. I knew some Spanish and knew that word meant beautiful. It was an even bigger compliment to a woman than "*linda*" or "*bella*". I didn't see how anything around here could be beautiful. We still couldn't see much because of the fog, and the stench of decay, while faint, still lingered.

138

Pepe moved to Mulo's side and dug through one of their bags. He soon produced two bandanas, one red and white, the other solid red. The older man took the solid one, and his son tied it to his wrist. The other bandana Gordo wrapped around his stocking cap. Pepe looked to me while gesturing to his bandana. "For good luck."

Satisfied with their new adornments, the men began walking again, Gordo dropping to the rear of the procession. Robert led Mulo, and of course, I went wherever the beast did.

Leaning back over the mule's neck to rest, when we approached what the others had been looking at, I saw a set of footprints, left by bare feet, going from the edge of the trail to the inside wall. I looked over my right shoulder and could see dirt disturbed on the bank inside the trail, presumably from when the person went up. But how could they climb that bank so easily? And why on earth would they be barefoot in this chilly temperature?

As we continued, I dozed again despite the pain. I let sleep envelop me, exhaustion depleting my will to stay awake.

A scream woke me, and I sat up quickly, which made me woozy. I put my hands on either side of Mulo's neck to steady myself, knowing my right leg would be no help in stopping me if I slid that way. Robert flew between me and the inside of the trail, barely missing my injured leg, and I turned to see where he was going.

Only the top half of Gordo was visible over the edge of the trail, and he clung with one hand to an exposed root. "*Papá! Papá! Papá!*" he yelled over and over as his other hand scrabbled to reach the same root.

When Robert reached Gordo, he froze, looking over the edge of the trail. The struggling guide managed to clutch Robert's pant leg in his fist, and he began to pull himself up. For some reason, Robert took a slow step back, breaking the grip on his pants.

Gordo quit struggling and looked to Robert, the guide's eyes wide and still. His mouth opened as if to speak, and we saw a clawed hand shoot up and bury its fingertips in Gordo's flank. Blood sprayed, and Gordo's mouth opened fully in a silent scream. He let go of the root and instantly fell from sight.

I looked at Robert, who stood in the same place, staring at the space where Gordo had been. Then he slowly turned toward me, adjusted his headlamp, and, of all things, smiled.

Up the trail from me, Pepe was speaking rapidly in Spanish, his hands alternating from forming the sign of the cross and making an X with his index fingers. "We must go back. Now."

He grabbed the mule's lead and tried to turn the animal around, but the trail was still too narrow. His gaze searched ahead of us, then he nodded sharply. "Around the bend, it is wider. We can turn there." Pepe took off toward the curve, pulling the animal and me behind him.

Just as we started moving, behind me I heard a soft "Yes." I turned, remembering Robert was still back there, and just as I started to speak, Pepe did so for both of us. "*Dios mío.*"

Standing just inches from Robert was a dark-skinned woman. Her black hair was long and thick, covering her entire body to her ankles. Through her thick mane I saw a single exposed nipple and just a hint of a pubic thatch. She was stunning, one of the most beautiful women I had ever seen, and I found myself getting aroused.

Then my eyes refocused on her feet. They were backward. Her knees pointed forward, but her feet, however impossible it might seem, pointed in the opposite direction. It dawned on me then why Pepe had formed the X over the ledge below us. The creature had gone down the bank, not up.

While my mind registered this fact, it was almost immediately pushed to the background as I again returned my gaze to the naked parts of her form I could see. I licked my lips, wishing I was in Robert's place where I could admire her beauty more closely.

"*Ciguapa,*" Pepe whispered, now standing beside me. "*Dios mío, una ciguapa.*"

Robert lifted his hands then stopped, looking at the woman's face. She nodded, and his hands continued, caressing her breasts. His smile broadened, and he leaned closer to her.

"Robert," I called, but his attention never wavered. The same could not be said for the woman.

Her head snapped sideways, and her eyes held me. While I watched, her expression, for lack of a better phrase, rippled. The face of the beautiful woman disappeared, looking for a moment like water a rock had been dropped in, then calmed again. I wished it hadn't.

Now her face was long, her chin extended midway down her chest. Most of her head was a dark maw with sharp fangs throughout. A flat, almost non-existent nose sat between that mouth and her eyes, which shone like blood-red moons.

The creature's attention returned to Robert, whose face instantly transformed to a rictus of horror. Her hands rose to his shoulders, and those long claws reappeared, burying themselves in my son's shoulders. Rivulets of blood ran down his chest and torso.

In a movement I barely perceived, the ciguapa's mouth was suddenly enveloping the side of Robert's neck, closing on it. She shook her head from side-to-side like a wild dog with a rabbit. Blood flowed freely down my son's chest, but he stayed motionless.

I couldn't speak. I couldn't move. I could barely even think.

Pepe, however, had no such problems. As he passed the mule, he slid a shiny machete from its sheath and stepped toward the creature. A visceral scream escaped him as he covered the distance in two quick steps and swung the blade downward.

The machete cut deeply between her neck and shoulder, splitting the muscle and exposing part of the collarbone. She did not stop, barely even registering the attack.

Down came the blade again, this time slicing deep into her neck. The ciguapa's body shook, and she pulled briefly from Robert's neck, a torrent of gore and flesh pouring from her fangs. Without waiting, Pepe freed the machete and swung it down once more, this time with both hands.

The creature's head was separated, and her body dropped to the trail in a heap. Her claws were still entrenched in Robert's shoulders, and he fell with her. Both were still.

Our remaining guide slowly walked toward me, and as he resheathed the blade, I noticed it was still as clean as it had been when he'd drawn it. Silently the man returned to the bodies on the trail and without ceremony dragged them to the edge of the trail. Placing a

141

booted foot against them, he pushed the pile until it went over the edge. I saw my son for the last time as he disappeared, still in the creature's clutches.

Pepe, looking so much older than when we had started, stared at the *ciguapa's* head where it lay on the trail. Then he took a couple steps back, moved forward, and swung his leg against the head as if he were a soccer player launching his best corner kick. The remainder of the *ciguapa* flew an impressive distance before darkness overtook it. I heard but did not see it land below.

I watched Pepe as he worked his way back in front of me, removed his headlamp, wiped his brow with his sleeve, and replaced the light on his head.

"Now we go back."

Author Notes

Most anthologies don't have stories with international settings, much less two in somewhere as specific as the Dominican Republic. But here we are.

This is actually based on an actual Dominican legend, that of the ciguapa. How they are described varies, but one consistent feature is the backward-facing feet. They are said to live in the mountains of the Dominican Republic, seducing men like sirens and leading them to their deaths.

Pico Duarte is actually the highest peak not only in the Dominican Republic but in the Caribbean as a whole. Naturally, there are many people who wish to conquer it and get their sunrise selfie next to the bust of Juan Pablo Duarte, one of the founding fathers of Dominican independence.

I don't remember where I first learned of the ciguapa, but it's a fascinating legend. Most of the research on this, besides reading about the legend of the creature itself, was watching YouTube videos of those who've conquered the peak. The places where they establish a base camp and stop midway are both part of one of the routes up the mountain.

BERT EDENS

"Deadwood"

Adam loved the aroma of burning flesh. Both Hernandez twins from down the street had smelled like cherry wood. His father, hickory. And Adam's estranged wife, Corinne, the intoxicating fragrance of maple.

As he stoked the flames in the fireplace, Adam inhaled deeply the smoke rolling from the fire, letting it saturate his nose and throat and lungs. He had partially closed the flue to fill his house, the low ceiling of smoke burning and stinging his eyes. Tears of joy flowed down his cheeks.

He was making His Oak happy.

The mighty tree stood deep in the forest, towering above the rest of the thicket. Yes, they may have been mature but were insignificant, mere acorns in importance. Adam's Oak, it was the strongest and tallest, destined to be the sole survivor, as was Adam.

A couple weeks ago, Corinne had gotten pissed at him, just because he had shattered a bowl of stew against the wall, claiming it was the final straw, and started packing a suitcase. Adam was no Einstein, but he knew when he needed to take a walk. So, walk he did. Out the back door and through their yard, bordered on three sides by an unfinished privacy fence, to the forest behind their property.

Weaving between the trees, stepping over felled trunks, jeans stained green by moss and Nikes caked with mud, Adam made his way into the forest. Head down, picking his way, he felt a weight lift from him as his anger drifted away with the breeze and fluttering butterflies.

Soon, his entire field of vision was filled by a single trunk. Adam raised his eyes and studied the magnificent specimen in front of him.

Limbs drooped far on either side of him, but there were none within reach while standing next to the base. Even if he climbed onto one of the massive roots and jumped, he still couldn't reach the nearest one.

Adam walked a circle around the tree, awed by its girth. After making a couple trips, he counted his paces as he rounded it again. Twenty-four. That put the circumference of this beast at about seventy-five feet, and Adam guessed it was at least that tall. Amazing.

Settling on the ground beside the oak, Adam leaned against it. The rough bark poked and scratched his back, but he rubbed against it like livestock would, enjoying the texture and slight pain of the motion. He closed his eyes and lost himself in the forest. The distant chatter of a mockingbird, the rich loamy smell of the dirt and rotted leaves around him. Adam sighed and pushed against the tree, digging his heels into the earth.

Closer.

Adam's eyes flickered open. He scanned the woods around him but saw nobody.

Yes, Adam. Closer. The voice was deep but scratchy, muffled as if talking through a mouthful of cotton. Or leaves.

This time, as the voice echoed in his head, Adam could feel vibrations in his back, mirroring the words.

You are mine, and I am yours, Adam. Only we can understand each other.

Scrambling to his feet, he eyed the huge tree. His hand moved slowly toward the tree until his palm rested against it. *Yes,* came the reply to his silent question, the nerves in his arm electric with the word.

Adam blinked a couple times and looked around him again. "I must be losing my fucking mind," he mumbled as he tangled his fingers in his thick brown hair and scratched his scalp, flurries of dandruff floating to his shoulders.

Nobody understands us, Adam. We are but two among a forest of weaklings, saplings bent under the weight of their own existence.

Pacing in front of the giant tree, Adam chewed his fingernails and worked his jaw. Finally, he stopped and looked to the oak's canopy. "Why—. Why me?"

You need not speak out loud for me to hear you, Adam. We are the same.

"I'm definitely losing my fucking mind," Adam muttered while staring at the limbs high above him. A deep breath escaped him, and he closed his eyes. "What the hell," he said. *What do you want with me?* he thought, afraid to open his eyes.

Immortality, Adam. You and I can live forever, the foundation legends are built upon.

"Yeah, like that helps me think I'm sane," Adam mumbled and walked back to his house.

When he stepped back inside, he noticed Corinne had set her suitcase beside the front door, as if to say "I am *this* close, mother-fucker" but was bustling about the kitchen fixing dinner. Adam sat on a barstool at the kitchen island and watched her chop onions. As she was working on mushrooms and garlic, Adam told her of his experience in the woods.

"You've lost your fucking mind," she told him flatly and went back to abusing the vegetables on the cutting board, her knife working faster and more violently.

"Well, at least we agree on something," he said and changed the subject to her work. Corinne was an LPN at their local medical center and often rotated shifts as needed. Adam didn't like her being gone during graveyard shifts, but the differential pay helped them keep ahead of their mortgage payments.

After their first communication, His Oak was silent for several days, and Adam made no more trips to the forest. Corinne's suitcase eventually made its way back to the bedroom closet, but she never emptied it. He tried to make love to her a couple times, but each time she firmly moved his hands or pushed his face away. She was a Scorpio, and Adam knew she'd let him back inside her walls whenever she was damn well ready. But, being a guy, he had to at least try. Just in case, you know.

One night, just after Adam had returned to bed from taking a piss, the voice in his head returned. *It's time, Adam.*

He sat up quickly and looked at Corinne. Her back was to him, as usual, but she didn't move. "Wha—," he started to say, then remembered he could project thoughts to the tree. *What do you mean, it's time?*

147

If a voice in his head could release an exasperated sigh, that's what Adam heard. *Immortality, Adam. Immortality.*

Yeah, you're gonna have to elaborate a bit, Adam thought.

You are tied to me, Adam. Your mind, life, and soul. As you die, I die. As I die, so do you. And we both deserve immortality.

Well, I've always said I'm potentially immortal until proven otherwise, but I still don't know what you're trying to say. Adam climbed from bed and slipped out to the living room, careful to close the door quietly behind him.

He sat in silence on the sofa for several minutes and was about to give up and go back to bed when the voice returned. *It's a competition, Adam. We all fight for our own existence. There is only so much oxygen for humans to breathe, and there's only so much carbon dioxide for us.*

But you see, Adam, as there are more people on the earth, there is less room for trees. Man does not understand how it works. As they bulldoze a tree in the Amazon, a woman in France may die, so nobody sees the connection. Saplings appear as babies are born, but the rate you humans reproduce outpaces our growth, and soon we will have no earth remaining to spread our roots. Or it will be poisoned by the factories and waste man produces.

Silence filled Adam's head again as he waited for more information. When none came, he asked, *So what do I need to do?*

Thin the forest, Adam. Thin the forest.

I need to cut down trees?

No, Adam. You need to cut down people.

Half-asleep, it took a moment for Adam to register what the tree had told him. "I need to … kill them," he said, not realizing his words were out loud.

Yes. For us to stand alone forever, you must remove any obstacles to our breathing.

"I can't just kill people. The cops will bust through my door and haul my ass off. Some tree in Kenya may die, but that's all I'll get accomplished." Adam paced the living room, hands in motion in front of him as if conducting an orchestra. "This is ridiculous."

No, Adam, it is destiny. Yours, mine, ours. We are fated to be the sole survivors. We need no others.

"Yeah, but killing folks? Shit, that's crazy talk." Adam stopped walking and furrowed his brow. "Hell, it's crazy just talking to some tree like you were kicked back in my recliner enjoying a cold brew." He restarted his pacing, head shaking.

As Adam reached the edge of the living room, he noticed Corinne standing in the hallway outside their bedroom, a look of disgust on her face. Without a word, she turned and left, Adam on her heels.

"Hey, babe, sorry I woke you," he said, false buoyancy filling his voice.

"I can't do this, Adam. You need to figure out whatever the hell is going on with you." Corinne pulled her suitcase from the closet, opened it, and tossed in more underwear and t-shirts. "I'm heading to Megan's. You call me when this shit is sorted out."

Adam side-stepped between Corinne and the door. "Babe, you're still in your nightgown and barefoot. Come on back to bed."

"Move. Your. Ass."

"But—"

"Move it. Now." No anger, no inflection, just demand. Her eyes showed no emotion. Adam stepped aside.

He followed Corinne as she grabbed the keys to her Honda Accord from beside the garage door but didn't follow her to the car. She slid inside, still barefoot, and left without looking back at Adam.

Once again, the tree was silent for several more days. Adam called in sick to work the first two days and was thankful when the weekend arrived, so he wouldn't have to explain his absence to anyone.

Since Corinne left, Adam had filled his belly with vodka and his mind with hatred. And every bit of anger was directed at himself.

Adam was weak. He knew it without question; that was why Corinne had left. But he would not be pushed around anymore. A better class of woman needed to be in his life, and Adam was going to make it happen. And he knew just who could help him.

A plan of attack now in place, Adam reached out to the tree with his mind. *Help me. Tell me what I need to do, how I can be stronger.*

The rustling voice instantly boomed in Adam's mind. *Prove yourself. You have been weak and let the woman control you. Show me you are worthy to stand beside me for eternity.*

Adam topped off his tumbler with Smirnoff and dropped onto his couch, splashing alcohol on his shirt. He took a deep draw from the glass, savoring the burn on his tongue and throat and empty stomach. *How? What do I have to do?*

A sacrifice. You must show me you are willing to do what must be done for us, that nobody can stand in our way. You must not let emotion control you any longer.

But who? Adam asked.

That is your choice. Then silence.

Since a trip to the liquor store was in order so he could stock up on more fuel, Adam hopped into his car and headed that way. Just after he checked out, having bought a couple bottles of vodka and bourbon, Adam's phone rang.

"Hey, Adam, just checking to see how you're doing." It was his dad. "You hanging in there, since, well—" His voice trailed off, Corinne's departure implied but left unmentioned.

"Doing fine, Pop. Just out for some fresh air." Adam sat in the front seat of his car, door propped open and leg hanging out, rubbing a thumb across the cap of the Wild Turkey. Boy, did he want to open it and take a swig.

"Good, good. The 'Boys are playing the Steelers in the early game today, and you've got satellite to watch it. Mind if I pop by so we can catch it? They'll probably get their asses kicked, but hey, what the hell."

An idea formed in Adam's mind, and he smiled to himself. A lady leaving the liquor store saw him and waved, as if she thought he was flirting with her. "That would be good, Pop. Misery loves company and all that, huh?"

Adam drove home, hands clinched on the steering wheel the whole way. He caught himself holding his breath several times and had to consciously control it. "You can do this, man," he told himself. "You can prove yourself to Your Oak."

Once home, Adam scooted through the living room and kitchen, tidying as best he could. Last thing he wanted was a lecture from his dad about how shitty the house looked, as that would only drive home how much Corinne's absence was making a difference. And that would show weakness, something he didn't want to do right now.

Adam's dad arrived midway through the first quarter, Cowboys already down seven to nothing. He fixed himself a bourbon on the rocks and settled onto the couch. "Gee, they're losing, what a surprise," he yelled over his shoulder to Adam, who was leaning against the kitchen counter.

The son looked at his father and was at ease. No sweaty palms, no twitch in his hands, no increased breathing. He picked up his chef's knife with one hand and santoku with the other. Walking with a pace measured by purpose, Adam was soon standing behind his father, looking down at him.

"Shit, Adam, the 'Boys need a new running back. Fucker just fumbl—"

The man's rant was replaced by an agonizing scream as Adam buried a blade behind each collarbone. As he watched the Steelers celebrate the turnover, Adam twisted the blades as if revving the throttle on his Harley. "Gonna be another losing season. Of course," he muttered.

When his dad was still, Adam removed the knives and went to the kitchen. He cleaned and dried the blades with loving care and placed them in the knife block.

Returning to the living room, Adam eyed the tree he had felled, sap pouring from it and staining his furniture. He knew he had to take care of it, if only to reclaim his couch. A quick trip to his woodshed later, Adam had his ax in hand. Fortunately, with it being fall, he had kept the blade sharp so he'd have a good supply of firewood for the winter.

Adam dragged the tree to the middle of the room, stopping to watch the Cowboys' quarterback crumple under a defensive lineman. "Figures," he mumbled and brought the ax down. It struck at the joint of one of the smaller limbs, but all it did was flex in the middle. He tried again but got the same result.

Remembering the lumberjack competitions he'd seen on ESPN, Adam stepped on each end of the limb to hold it still and swung the ax. Two more chops, and the limb was halved.

It took about an hour for Adam to successfully transform the tree into kindling. The hardest part was isolating the trunk, and he had to take a break to catch his breath and watch the rest of the ass-beating on TV.

While he sat on the now-red couch, licking and savoring the sticky-sweet sap on his hands, Adam reached out with his mind to His Oak. *How am I doing?*

Silence.

Adam pondered for a minute and realized he hadn't finished the job. What else do you do with a nice pile of kindling besides burn it?

So, he rose from the couch and began stacking the wood in the fireplace. He started with the trunk on the bottom, since it was the biggest piece and would make the best base. Then he criss-crossed the limbs across the trunk, careful to maintain the balance. Finally, he set the last piece, a ball-shaped chunk of wood, at the peak.

As he looked at the final piece, Adam decided the two knotholes would look better bare. So, he flicked open his pocketknife and removed the bark covering them. There. Much better.

Adam tried several times to light the firewood, but it was just too wet. Grabbing a gasoline container from his garage, he doused the pile of kindling. Stepping back a couple feet, he lit a match and tossed it into the fireplace. Flame erupted into the living room, the heat wrinkling the big-screen TV on the mantel. "Shit," Adam said, "now I have to replace it."

The kindling finally began burning, and the room was filled with smoke. Adam inhaled deeply. *Hickory*, he thought. Memories of his childhood crept into Adam's mind. His father used to take him camping and hunting, a tradition they maintained from the time Adam was eight until he graduated high school.

One skill his father had taught him was identifying wood by the aroma of the smoke. Every time they were in the woods, Adam's dad would grab dead branches around the campfire, toss them in, and make Adam close his eyes and identify the type of tree.

It was one of Adam's favorite memories of his dad. As the blaze broke down the firewood, sap bubbling and sizzling, Adam wondered why his dad hadn't stopped by in a long time. Maybe he should call him so they could go camping again. It had been several years now.

Four hours passed before the flames in the fireplace had run out of fuel and fizzled out. Adam spent an hour with a paring knife, whittling away the excess bark and burnt sap, happy when he had mostly clean wood remaining. As he pondered what to do with it, Adam watched through the wrinkled TV screen a soccer match between France and the United States.

Then he remembered a YouTube video about the catacombs under Paris, where literally millions of bones had been stacked in an effort to thin overcrowded cemeteries. That's what he needed, an homage to the mission for His Oak.

Reaching out to the great tree in his thoughts, Adam hoped for some confirmation he was on the right path, doing what he must to ensure their immortality. But only silence greeted him.

"I'm not finished yet," Adam said while scratching his chin. He went to the front porch and dumped out a bucket full of That Bitch Corinne's begonias, rinsing it out with a water hose. Then he filled it with the burnt kindling and headed to his shop building.

There he cleared a corner of tools and potting soil, then he stacked the wood neatly in a pile, the largest ones on the bottom and the odd round-shaped one on top. Standing back, he admired the first steps of his project. *Not a bad start*, he thought.

Killing someone near the end of life is easy, echoed the voice of His Oak in Adam's head, *but you must prove you are willing to take the young and innocent too. Old, rotted trees fall easily, but green saplings take more effort.*

Adam nodded and considered this as he went back inside. He grabbed the poker and shovel and began clearing away the mess remaining in the fireplace. He was about thirty minutes into the work when the doorbell rang. Walking to the door, poker still in hand, Adam found Maria and Tina Hernandez, the twins from four houses down.

"Mr. Jensen, would you like to buy some candy bars?" Maria asked him. Or was it Tina? Adam could never tell them apart, and the fact they wore matching blue soccer uniforms and white headbands didn't help.

"What are they for?" he asked, resting the fireplace poker on his shoulder. "I'm happy to support you, but you have to give me the full spiel."

The twins looked at each other and shrugged, and the one who hadn't spoken yet, whichever she was, responded in a measured, practiced rhythm. "We are raising money to go to the national tournament in Fort Walton Beach, Florida. Our team is undefeated in eleven matches, and our coach thinks we have a really good chance to make it." She beamed after she had finished.

"That was pretty good. How old are you girls?"

"Ten," they answered in unison and giggled.

"Well, it seems like a good cause. But what if you don't make it? Can I get a refund?"

They exchanged glances and more shrugs. "I'm just kidding," Adam said, his smile not quite reaching his eyes. "It's not like I can give you the chocolate back. Come on in, I need to get my wallet from the bedroom."

He stepped to the side and let the girls inside. They froze when they saw the red-stained couch, the wood floor looking much the same, with countless nicks and divots caused by Adam's ax.

Adam didn't give them a chance to fully process the scene. He swung the poker with his best tennis backhand swing, catching one twin above the left ear. She dropped immediately, and her sister spun to look at Adam.

The forehand swing caught her, the hook at the end of the poker lodging in her temple with a sucking *thoock*. Her legs gave out and urine ran down the inside of one thigh. Adam tried to support her weight with the tool, but gave up and lowered her to the floor. Putting one foot on her neck, he rocked the poker, trying to free it, but it was stuck.

"Come on, oh … whichever the fuck twin you are. Let go," he muttered. Finally, he was able to free it by using the tip like the claw on a hammer, leverage forcing the hook loose, skull fragments raised in adoration of Adam's mission for His Oak.

He dragged the saplings to the middle of the living room floor and began chopping them into kindling. Adam had learned much with the first felling, and it took him little time to cut the first tree into small pieces. Wiping sweat from his brow, he smeared sap across his face in the process. But Adam was unfazed. He had work to do.

Just as Adam stood over the remaining tree and firmly placed a foot on each end of one limb, its knotholes opened. Adam didn't notice and brought the ax down, splitting the limb in half. Screeching filled the room, and he covered his ears with his hands.

"Fucking birds!" he yelled. Turning toward the noise, Adam swung his ax at the top of the tree, determined to scare away the screaming birds. The ax split the canopy on the first swing, and only the sound of his chopping remained. But Adam didn't stop, hacking at the top of the tree over and over and over, until it was in the size of pieces he wanted.

"Finally. Shit." He turned his attention to the TV, watching a commercial for Mr. Clean. Looking about the room, Adam decided he might need to get something to clean up all the bark, sap, and wood chips. Well, that would have to be later, he decided, and went back to work.

As before, he stacked the kindling in the fireplace and lit it. Fortunately, these limbs were much smaller and were reduced to just the wood core in much shorter time. The house filled with the sweet scent of cherry wood, and he smiled to himself. Marvelous.

While he waited, Adam cleaned his ax in the sink, took a shower, and put on clean clothes. He contemplated putting on his Cowboys jersey, but considering how the fuckers had played today, opted for an Alice Cooper concert t-shirt paired with faded jeans.

Adam renewed the flames in the fireplace with another toss of gasoline and went outside to check the mail. He was halfway down the sidewalk when he remembered it was Sunday. Oh yeah. No mail today.

Then he spotted the identical white bicycles parked in front of the holly bushes lining his front porch. Those damn kids down the road had left their bikes just laying around again. Last time they'd done that, he had returned them to their house.

This time, Adam decided he'd teach the little shits a lesson. He grabbed the bikes, walked to the side of the house, and tossed them over his privacy fence into his backyard. *There*, he thought, *good luck finding them now.*

Back inside, Adam waited until the fire had burned itself out, then he cleaned the wood with his paring knife as before. Even with two saplings, they didn't fill up as much of the bucket as the first one had. He took the remnants and stacked each tree in adjacent piles, one with the round piece neatly on top, the other stacked with the fragments of wood chips.

Adam tried to contact His Oak with his mind, but it was a while before an answer came. All it said was, *Be careful. Not all appreciate our mission.*

Knowing he didn't have much time until the Eagles and Giants game later, Adam popped some pizza rolls into the oven and set about neatening up the living room. His couch looked like Corinne had spilled some Cabernet or something on it, so he just tossed the wedding quilt her grandmother had made them over the red. Plopping down on the couch, Adam was channel surfing when the doorbell rang again.

At the door was a police officer, dressed in black except for the shiny silver badge and name plate. CROUCH, it said. As Adam opened the door, the policeman's hand slid to his sidearm, his palm resting lightly on the handle.

"Evening, sir, I'm Sergeant Crouch with Elaine Police Department. Mr. and Mrs. Hernandez down the street called us when their ten-year-old girls didn't come back home after going door-to-door, selling chocolate bars for their soccer team. Have you seen them?" His gaze fixed on Adam, eyes darting around his face as if looking for evidence or tells of guilt.

"Yes, sir, they were here a while ago, but it's been a couple hours." Adam thought of the abandoned bikes and held the officer's stare, his expression appropriately solemn. *Poor little girls*, he thought. *Sure hope they're okay.*

"Did you buy anything from them?" the officer continued and sniffled, wiping his nose. "Sorry, cold."

"I'm sorry, officer, those suck. And no, all I had was my debit card, and they said they didn't have a Square or any other way to take a card payment." Adam scratched behind his ear, the officer sliding one foot back slightly at the sudden movement. "I told them if they came back tomorrow night, after I got home from work, I could hit the ATM at lunch and get some cash." As Adam spoke, the officer leaned to the side to peek behind Adam into the living room, but if he saw anything, his expression didn't register it.

"Normally, I keep a twenty in my wallet in case I needed gas and the credit card readers at the gas pumps are down. But not this time." Adam shrugged. "I had to use it at the Quick Mart on Woods Street last Wednesday and used the rest getting some King Size Payday bars. Love 'em," he added as he patted his belly. "A little too much, in fact."

Officer Crouch studied for a moment the grin presented to him then nodded. "Well, if you see anything that might be a clue, call 911. No sense calling the non-emergency number. We need to find these girls."

"Yes, sir, I will. I'll also tell my wife when she gets home, so she can keep an eye out too."

"Thank you, sir, have a good day." The officer nodded at Adam and walked to his cruiser parked at the curb. Adam watched until the police car had moved to the next house, then he closed the door.

Pizza rolls cooked, Adam piled them onto a plate, grabbed a Budweiser from the fridge, and settled onto the couch to watch the game. By the time he had finished the pile of food, Adam had scorched the inside of his mouth several times with the molten contents. But it was all worth it. He loved pizza rolls, especially the pepperoni ones.

Midway through the first quarter, the door burst open and Corinne charged in. "Don't you fucking knock?" Adam asked her.

"It's still my house too, asshole," Corinne retorted. "I need to pick up more of my stuff." Then her eyes settled on the damaged wood floor. "What the fuck did you do, Adam? And what is that awful smell?" Her forehead and nose wrinkled.

"I burned the pizza rolls. You know I can't cook for shit."

"Yeah, that ain't it." Corinne pointed to the floor then flapped a hand at him. "Whatever. You're paying to have that fixed, not me," she snapped then stalked to the bedroom. Adam put his plate in the kitchen and followed her.

"Hey, bitch, that's my suitcase," he said when he saw her packing more clothes. "You can't take that."

"I'm just using it to get more of my shit out of here. Believe me, I don't want anything of yours." Corinne grabbed another handful of panties and socks. "I'll drop it back off tomorrow. Just stick it inside the front door or something."

Corinne disappeared into the closet, bumping his tie rack on the door. Half its contents fell to the floor. Adam picked up several and was staring at one of his Looney Tune ties when Corinne stalked past him, bumping him with her shoulder. He fiddled with the tie, already in a loop, as he didn't know how to tie them. Like a good wife, at least at that time, Corinne had helped him tie each one, then he would just loosen it enough to slip over his head.

She started folding her blouses and rolling them into tight packages to fit as many as possible into the suitcase. As she worked at her task, Adam stole behind her, rubbing her ass with his crotch. "Oh hell no," Corinne spat. Bolting upright, she started to turn, but the tie was already around her neck.

Adam encircled the knot with his thumb and forefinger and pushed against her neck with that hand. The other he jerked back as if starting a lawnmower. A sharp gasp escaped Corinne's throat, and her hands shot up to relieve the pressure. She never got the chance.

Dragging her backward, Adam reached over the top of the closet door with the hand holding the end of the tie. Then, with Corinne safely on the other side, he grabbed the tie with both hands and leaned all his weight away from the door.

Corinne slid up the door a couple feet, hands still desperately trying to find purchase beneath the garrotte, succeeding only in tearing her own flesh. Blood ran down her neck and buried deep under her fingernails as she struggled. She flailed with her feet, heels thudding multiple holes in the cheap door.

Meanwhile, Adam continued leaning his weight back, waiting for the struggling to subside, admiring the quality and strength of an eight-dollar Wal-Mart tie. Soon, stillness and silence overtook the room, and he let the burden at the end of the tie down.

Stepping to the other side of the door, Adam freed the tie, its work for the day done. He studied where it had become frayed while stretched across the top of the door. Shaking his head Adam made a mental note to see if he could find another just like it, maybe on Amazon. He couldn't very well wear that one to work. He'd look like shit.

Adam dragged the newly felled tree to his workspace in front of the fireplace. Nothing interesting was on TV, so he switched it off and began chopping the wood. By this point, his arms and shoulders ached, and his hands were blistering. But he had to finish the job.

Firewood piled into the the fireplace, Adam splashed the last of the gasoline on the stack. It wouldn't nearly be enough to complete the job, and he'd have to run to the Quick Mart to get more, but at least it would get the job started.

He closed the flue to force all the smoke into the house so he could revel in its aroma. Tossing a match on the pile, it burst into flames. The sweet, heavenly aroma of maple filled his nostrils. Adam's eyes burned and stung, but he didn't care. Tears of joy streamed down his face. He was fulfilling his mission.

He was making His Oak happy.

A flash of light caught Adam's attention, and his reverie was shattered. The front room was flooded with blue lights. The voice in Adam's head was immediate, booming, and insistent. *Run. Run to me.*

Adam shot through the house and burst out the back door. He ran. Not knowing where to, not thinking, just following instinct. His footsteps were sure, his balance perfect, and he soon found himself at the base of His Oak. He pressed his chest and cheek to the great trunk. *What do I do now?*

Silence.

Please, you must help me. You've been my anchor, my reason for everything I've done. We should be together forever. Please help me.

But there was nothing from the tree. Far away, Adam heard faint shouts.

Looking at the branches high above the trunk, Adam knew he couldn't scale the tree, even in his youth. His eyes followed the path of several branches until he found one that almost reached the ground at the edge of the canopy. It looked strong enough, and Adam hurried to it.

It took a couple jumps before Adam was able to grab a thicker part of the branch. Under his weight, it bowed to the ground, and he walked hand-over-hand until the strength of the limb forced him to tip-toe. Gripping tightly with his hands, Adam swung his feet up and wrapped them around the wood. Looking like a sloth, he worked his way up the branch toward the center of the tree.

Near the trunk, another branch crossed under Adam, and he was able to put his weight on it and began climbing branches, higher and higher into the tree. Below him, flashlights played across the ground, a multitude of voices following them.

As he stepped across a branch, Adam's foot knocked some leaves loose, and they fluttered below, landing on a policeman at the base of the tree. The officer soon found Adam with his flashlight and yelled, "Hey, stop. Come on down. We just want to talk."

Adam looked down at the man and paused, catching his breath. After chopping wood all day, the last thing he needed to do was climb a tree. But here he was, thirty feet in the air, hands bleeding from burst blisters, forearms and cheeks scratched, shoulders and neck screaming at him in their fatigue.

"Something happened in your house, and we just want to talk about it," the officer shouted. "Or if you want, we can have the fire department get a ladder out here to get you down." Other policemen joined him, and the canopy around Adam was bathed in light.

The branch above Adam was just about eye level, but the next closest one above that was eight or nine feet more. There was no way he could get any higher.

Help me, he pleaded with His Oak. But it rebuked him with its silence. Had it ever talked to him? Adam pondered the times he had begged it for guidance today, but none had come. Was he just stressed from his fight with Corinne? Could he have done this all on his own?

Adam inched toward the trunk until he could press his chest and cheek and palms to it. There he balanced on the limb, begging for the beautiful vibration he had felt from the tree the first time it had talked to him. Adam begged. Pleaded. Cried.

But there was nothing. No motion from the tree other than what the wind coaxed from it, and no voices except those below.

Tears poured down Adam's cheeks as he leaned his back against the trunk. All the tree felling he had done today was for naught. Nothing was to be gained except derision from the public and justice system. He would be a pariah.

His eyes found a V in the branch near his head, and Adam moved toward it. Holding onto the branch with one hand, he loosened his belt with the other. Adam reached above him to use his forearms to balance against the limb.

Running the tip of the belt through the buckle, he tied the end to the branch as tight into the V as he could. As he did this, the activity below him, accompanied with frantic shouting, picked up as officers worked to find a way up to Adam. They spoke, but Adam didn't hear.

A few hard tugs on the belt assured Adam it was secure, and he looped the other end around his neck. Looking through the canopy, he could see a dark smoke pouring from the back door of his house. Just beyond that, a gaggle of police cars flashed their lights as they blocked the street.

Adam wished he could say goodbye to Corinne. He'd really out-kicked his coverage with her, and she didn't deserve him. He hoped she would understand.

Closing his eyes, Adam stepped toward his home and fell, the sudden stop snapping his neck. As life fled Adam, all branches on His Oak lifted ever so slightly as if in victory.

☠ ☠ ☠

Four miles away, Tommy Greene peered through the oven door, watching the cheese melt on the garlic bread. His momma made the best garlic cheese bread, and he couldn't wait to have some. He peered around the kitchen island, bumping his head on the corner of the countertop.

Rubbing his forehead, Tommy called, "Mom? When the bread ready?" She didn't answer, and Tommy didn't hear the quiet footsteps heading his way.

161

Tommy turned back to the oven and grabbed the handle. He pulled on it, but the door barely budged. Putting his feet against the bottom of the appliance, he leaned back, and the door popped open, causing Tommy to lose his balance.

As he scrambled to regain his footing, both hands found the inside of the oven door, the subsequent sizzle of searing flesh immediately followed by screams of pain. Tommy's mother snatched him up quickly, clutching him to her chest, cooing soothing and comforting words to her son.

Just as Tommy settled down, his father walked into the kitchen, sniffed, and said, "Babe, did you fire up the smoker? Is that mesquite?"

Author Notes

The origin of this story was a writer workshop I did several years ago. There wasn't a submission goal at the end, just improving our writing style in what was essentially an online writer group with two seasoned mentors.

Originally, the prompt for the story we needed to write related to nature and its interactions with people. Of course, everyone in the group was a horror writer, so the stories all were in that vein. When I came up with this idea, it seemed to gather a lot of praise from the other writers, so I rolled with it and have tweaked it off and on since then.

I'm not sure where the idea of each person having a distinct wood aroma when burned came from, but it's a favorite of mine. Most of it just developed from bits and pieces of things I've read or ideas that occurred to me.

I will say that as a lifelong Pittsburgh Steelers fan, the ineptitude of the Dallas Cowboys in this story was almost mandatory. I mean, if the characters are going to gripe about anyone, it might as well be a team I dislike.

About the Author

Bert is an author and editor who has always been one to read anything put in front of him, a passion he still enjoys, reading in all genres. Long ago, when text-based browsers still roamed the earth, he had many short pieces published on various webzines that no longer exist, covering genres from non-fiction to horror to sci-fi to erotica. He also had a non-fiction story about his older son published in a collection of stories about premature babies.

Then life raising said older son, as well as the implied younger son, interceded, and he found little time to write. Now, as his sons are adults, he has begun finding more time to write. He has recently been published in multiple anthologies of flash fiction as well as in a magazine dedicated to supporting children with special needs. He also has multiple non-fiction and fiction pieces accepted for future publication.

When not writing, he is active as a martial arts instructor, software developer, an amateur chef, and a strong proponent for disability rights and empowerment of women. You are just as likely to find him in front of a keyboard, on a martial arts mat, baking banana bread, or sitting cross-legged in a used bookstore soaking up the bibliophilic aroma and feeding his addiction for rare or unusual cookbooks.

He lives in Arkansas with Carrie, a.k.a My Gorgeous Bride, the wife he doesn't deserve; his older son, Zak; two Corgis who rightly believe they are royalty; and a lovable but spoiled brat of a toy poodle.

If you feel so inclined, drop him a note at bert@bert-edens.com

Milton Keynes UK
Ingram Content Group UK Ltd.
UKHW042224140224
437801UK00005B/394